Nils

Nils

BREAKAWAY HOCKEY #3

S.R. GREY

Nils (Breakaway Hockey #3)
Copyright © 2024 by S.R. Grey

ISBN-13 (print edition): 979-8-9866072-7-6

Editing: Hot Tree Editing
Proofreading: Deaton Author Services
Beta Readers: Franci N. and JoAnna E.
Cover Photographer: Wander Aguiar Photography
Model: Blake Vargo
Cover Design: Najla Qamber
Formatting:

emtippettsbookdesigns.com

Books by
S.R. GREY

Judge Me Not series
I Stand Before You
Never Doubt Me
Just Let Me Love You
The After of Us

Inevitability duology
Inevitable Detour
Inevitable Circumstances

Promises series
Tomorrow's Lies
Today's Promises

A Harbour Falls Mystery trilogy
Harbour Falls
Willow Point
Wickingham Way

Laid Bare novella series
Exposed: Laid Bare 1
Unveiled: Laid Bare 2
Spellbound: Laid Bare 3
Sacrifice: Laid Bare 4

Chapter

One

ELLIE

Only a hundred more miles to Atlanta, Georgia—my destination—and that's when the rain begins. And by rain, I mean a deluge.

Great.

Flipping the wipers on in my silver Jaguar XF, a generous gift from my professional hockey player brother, Arden, I mutter, "This sucks."

I'm not a fan of driving in the rain on the interstate, especially when it's dark out. I had a bad experience once when I was driving in a storm and started to spin out. I regained control before anything really bad happened, but it's still something I don't like to think about.

This rain, though, brings it to the forefront of my thoughts, and, swallowing hard as I try to calm my racing heart, I slow down to below the speed limit.

Yeah, that's better.

But really, I think it's time to pull over.

Focusing solely now on getting off the road to wait out what is turning into a wicked thunderstorm, I flip on the blinker, ease my car over into the far-right lane, and take the next exit.

I'm lucky I'm just outside of Chattanooga, Tennessee, as I've been passing exit after exit. That's why it was easy to just take this one. If this storm had blown up in northern Georgia, exits would have been few and far between. I probably would have been forced to stay on the highway for a while.

Ugh!

Shuddering at that ominous thought, I drive down the exit lane and slow to a stop.

The traffic light swinging in the wind is red, so I have a minute to consider my options.

Okay, so there's a big gas station/convenience store located directly across the street. And there's a hotel on my left.

Let's see…

Well, I'm good on gas and snacks, and, since this appears to be only a passing storm, I won't be checking in anywhere for the night.

The hotel is out, but there's always food. I can easily grab a bite to eat at one of the many restaurants I see listed on the sign to my right. And—bonus!—I may be able to catch some of Arden's first game of the season.

My brother plays for the Atlanta Thunder, and their matchup tonight is against the Tampa Bay Lightning. It's the first game of the season for both teams and is being broadcast nationally. I tried to tune it in earlier on the car stereo, but all of the local stations were only playing music. And unfortunately, I let my Sirius XM subscription lapse, so the NHL channel was not an option.

I'm still disappointed about that, as it should be a good game.

The Lightning are the team that knocked the Thunder out of the first round of the playoffs this past spring.

Speaking of thunder and lightning, I hear an ominous rumble gathering steam. That sound becomes more like a damn freight train closing in as the sky around me lights up.

I better find a place to stop...and fast.

The restaurants listed on the sign appear to be mainly fast-food joints. But as I squint to see through the rain that's really pounding down now on my windshield, despite the wipers being on *high*, I spy a small sports bar tucked away behind the far side of the gas station, the one just across the street.

Perfect.

The light finally turns green, and I drive straight ahead to my destination. Of course, I hit a giant puddle along the way that sprays the sides of the car.

Yeah, didn't see that one.

Slowing down, I head into the sports bar parking lot.

I'm pumped when I notice there's a space right in front of the building, as the wooden overhang on the roof will shelter me from the rain. The parking lot is not exactly busy and bustling with people clamoring for places to park, but you bet your ass I pull into that open space so fast it's not even funny.

The rain is still pouring down furiously as I turn off the car. I have an umbrella in the trunk, but my suitcases are piled high on top of it. In the time it would take me to dig it out, I'm sure I'd get soaked.

May as well just hop out and sprint the few feet to get under the overhang.

That's what I do, but I still get a little wet. Good thing I have on a short trench coat over my jeans and navy blue boatneck top, as all in all I'm not too bad off.

Combing my fingers through my slightly damp, long raven-black hair, I blow out a breath and head for the entrance.

When I walk in, my eyes are immediately drawn to two big-screen TVs up on the wall behind the bar. Both are tuned in to the Thunder-Lightning game.

I smile.

I've chosen wisely.

I'll get to see some of my brother's game, after all.

I head to the bar and pull out a stool. The bartender, a good-looking guy with wide shoulders and caramel-colored hair, who appears to be around my age—twenty-three—strides over.

Wiping down the bar in front of me with a rag as I take a seat, he asks in a low drawl, "What can I get you, sweetheart?"

Okay, I know he's just trying to be nice and do his job, which I totally understand because, up until recently, I was waitressing at Applebee's all summer long while preparing to start law school.

Still, I'm not big on guys I don't know addressing me with terms of endearment.

I'd rather he just use my name, so I tell him, "Hey, I don't mean to be a jerk, but my name is Ellie, not sweetheart."

I smile so he knows this is nothing against him personally.

I think he gets it, as he raises his hands in a placating manner and says, "I'm sorry, miss. Er, I mean Ellie. I meant no offense."

"None taken," I assure him. "It's just a pet peeve of mine. But now that that's out of the way..." I let out a long sigh. "As for what you can get me, I'll have an iced tea and a menu, please."

Reaching under the bar, he slips out a glossy menu and, as he hands it to me, asks, "Would you like sweet tea or a Long Island iced tea?"

Wincing, as I'm really not trying to be difficult, but I think I'm coming off as such, I say, "Definitely nothing with alcohol. I have a long drive ahead of me still. Tea sounds good, but do you have any that's unsweetened?"

He shakes his head. "Nah, we only keep the sweetened stuff on hand. Sorry."

"That's okay," I say. "Just go ahead and give me that."

Rapping the bar once, he says, "You got it. One sweet tea coming up."

"Thanks," I murmur as he walks away.

Glancing up at the TV above the bar, I check out the game. The second period has just ended, and the score is 2-1.

That's good.

We have the lead.

Since it's intermission, I look away from the TV and down at the menu.

Apart from the few energy bars I had stowed away in my car for this trip, I haven't eaten anything since I left Chicago early this morning. To say I'm famished would be an understatement.

Unfortunately, food was the last thing on my mind for most of this drive. I've had plenty of other things to occupy my thoughts. But now that I'm perusing the selections on the menu—*just look at the accompanying mouthwatering photos!*—my stomach starts rumbling.

When the bartender returns with my glass of sweet tea, he asks me what I'd like to order.

Laughing, I say, "Can I have one of everything? It all looks so good."

That gets him to smile. "Hungry, are we?"

I nod vigorously. "Very. But in all seriousness, I'll go with a cheeseburger and fries."

He jots my order down on a notepad, and then asks, "Anything else? Our wings are really good. Nice and spicy. They're big too. They'll fill you up."

"No, thanks." I shake my head. "I do like wings with a kick, but the burger and fries should be enough."

Nodding, he walks away.

And now I wish he'd come back.

Or that the third period of the game would start.

Because all of those things that were weighing on my mind earlier are rushing back as fast as the rain is pounding down on the metal roof above us.

Things like…

I can't believe I dropped out of law school only one week into the fall semester.

Okay, in my defense, I did take a deferment, but still, I'm officially gone from the University of Chicago. At least, for now.

I'm actually gone from the whole city, seeing as I sublet my little furnished apartment for the remaining term of my lease.

So yeah, there's no going back to Chicago.

I knew I certainly was *not* going home to Toronto with my tail between my legs to stay with my parents. I told my brother, Arden, that, and because he knows where I'm at in my life—namely confused and unsure of what I want to do next—he generously offered for me to come to Atlanta and stay with him for a while in order to sort things out.

He's kind of an awesome brother like that, which is good since he's my only sibling.

I told him that I'm fine with the Atlanta part, as I could use a change of scenery, but I absolutely will not be staying at his house.

His girlfriend, Willow, just moved in recently, and I don't want to be that annoying third wheel, throwing a wrench into their new life together.

So yeah, no, I'm fine with living at one of those extended stay hotels, or something like that.

I told Arden how I felt, but he's not thrilled with my decision. Too bad, it is what it is. I am not bending on the accommodations situation.

Hell, I don't even know how long I want to stay in Atlanta. I guess it all depends on how things go. That would include my fun, throw-caution-to-the-wind little "side project."

Thinking about that project and who it involves makes me smile.

It also gives me a little thrill.

But there's no time to think about that now, as my burger and fries just arrived.

"Thanks," I tell the bartender as he sets the plate in front of me. "This looks delicious."

It really does too. The burger is juicy and huge, and the fries appear to be fresh cut ones.

"Enjoy," he says as he lifts a pitcher of sweet tea from behind the bar. "Would you like a refill on your drink, Ellie?"

Smiling, I check out his name tag, which I should have done earlier. "Sure, Jeff."

Chuckling and shaking his head, he refills my drink.

I thank him again, and he walks down along the bar to tend to other customers.

Taking a big bite out of my burger, which *is* freaking awesome, I set it back down on the plate and swipe my mouth with a paper napkin.

Looking up at the TV, I see the third period of the game is just getting underway.

The camera pans to the Thunder bench, and, hey, there's my

brother. Seeing him, even if it is only on the TV, makes me smile.

I'm excited to see him again in person.

But Arden isn't who I'm really looking for. No, it's the guy seated on the bench next to him—his teammate Nils Sten—who has captured my full attention.

Okay, I must confess—there's another reason why I really wanted to see this game. Arden can never know this, since they're not only teammates but best buds, but Nils is my secret crush.

He has been for a while, ever since I saw an interview with him, sans shirt, last season. He was all hot and sweaty, and I just kept imagining what it would feel like to run my hands down his smooth, hard chest and sculpted abs.

Oh, my!

Afterward, I watched tons more interviews with Nils. I also looked up articles. The good news is, at least for me, I know for sure he's not married, nor does he have a girlfriend.

It was okay to fantasize even more.

And fantasize I did.

My crush grew stronger, and that's how Nils became my secret "side project" for when I get to Atlanta.

That's right—I'm going to "have" that man in some way, shape, or form, even if it's only a onetime hookup.

I deserve this little bit of carefree fun. I've been leading such a serious life for so long, working my ass off all through college these past four years, getting straight A's, making the Dean's List and the Honors Society. Hell, I even worked a part-time job each and every summer.

My list of accomplishments could go on and on. That's why I was quickly accepted to one of the country's top law schools.

But then I realized I'm not sure if law is what I want to study…or if Chicago is really where I wanted to be.

I just don't know what I want to do. Go back to law school or do something else entirely?

I have no clue.

The only thing I do know for certain is that I freaking want Nils!

He's gorgeous, he's hot, he's tall, and he's made of freaking muscle. I love his wild, untamed dark blond hair, and the way he flips it back out of his face before he puts on his helmet.

Don't even get me started on his stunning green eyes. They're truly the color of emeralds.

Gah, kill me now.

I want to get lost in those eyes in person, while Nils does unspeakable things to me.

Oh, and the sinful things I'll do to him in return…

Sighing as I pop a fry into my mouth, I nod and assure myself that in this, I will win.

And I will, as Elena "Ellie" Troy always gets what she wants.

There's only one thing, a caveat, if you will—Arden can never know what I'm up to.

Chapter

Two

NILS

We win our home opener against the Tampa Bay Lightning. The victory is sweet, especially for my best friend and teammate, Arden Troy. Although nobody was holding it against him except himself, he made up for a bungled shot last season during the playoffs that took us out of contention.

Tonight, though, when confronted with that same shot, he nailed it. He scored in overtime, ensuring our victory.

Now everyone is in the locker room, high-fiving and congratulating him.

I already gave him a tap with my stick and a "Way to go, bro," as I passed by.

Now I'm seated next to Finn Norath, our second-line centerman, taking off my pads.

Finn, who has a rugged look about him that lets you know he just has to play some kind of a professional sport, tugs his black tech shirt over his head, making his reddish-brown hair stand up in all kinds of weird angles.

"Good to see Arden can finally put that playoff loss from last season behind him," he says.

"Yeah," I agree. "He was obsessing over it most of the summer."

"Until he met Willow," Finn says as he continues to undress. "She sure has been good for him."

"That's for sure," I concur.

It's true. Arden fell in love with our top-line center's sister last summer, and it's been the best thing for him. He's much more relaxed and happier these days. And now he can fully put the past behind him after his stellar play tonight.

Thinking about that winning shot, I say to Finn, "You know what? We should take Arden out to dinner tonight. We can make it like a celebration that he finally got the monkey off his back."

Standing, Finn grabs a thick white towel from the top shelf of his locker.

As he fluffs it out and wraps it around his waist, he says, "That's a great idea. Do you want to ask some of the other guys if they want to go too? Or should we just keep it the three of us?"

I shrug. "I think we should ask Hayden, for sure. But that's it. Arden will appreciate it more if we don't turn this into something too over the top. You know how he is, always trying to keep things low-key."

"Good point," Finn says. "So, do you want me to talk to Hayden, or are you going to?"

"I will," I say.

Nodding, he heads off to the showers.

I finish undressing and secure a towel around my waist. The showers are next for me, too, but I have one thing I need to do first.

Well, two things really.

I head across the locker room to check with Arden to make sure he's up for a late-night dinner. It'd suck if we were making plans and he didn't even want to go.

Lucky for us, he's in.

"Fuck, yeah," he says. "That will actually work out well."

"Yeah? How so?" I ask.

He explains, "My sister is coming into town late tonight. If we go to dinner, I should be back at the house right around the time she'll arrive. I want to be there and awake, 'cause Willow has to be up early for work tomorrow. She'll definitely be in bed by the time my sister rolls in."

"Ah, got it," I reply.

I now remember that Arden did say the other day that his little sister, who's having some kind of a post-college "I'm not sure what I want to do with my life" crisis, is moving into town.

"I forgot you told me she's coming in tonight," I go on. "What's her name again?"

"Elena," Arden replies. "But everyone just calls her Ellie."

"That's right." I nod, recalling he did tell me her name before. "Okay, well, we'll be sure not to keep you too long at the restaurant."

He laughs. "As long as I'm back by around midnight, I should be good."

"We'll definitely be out of the restaurant before then," I assure him.

I feel good as I walk away to take care of my next task. Finn and I clearly made the right decision to keep the dinner outing small. I wouldn't want Arden to miss Ellie's arrival, and if there were a bunch of us guys going out tonight, dinner would take much longer.

I stop by Hayden's locker next to see if he's up for going out tonight. The three of us are pretty tight, especially since we play together on the top line. Finn's been hanging out with us more lately, and he's been a good friend of mine for a while, so we're becoming a nice, little tight-knit group.

Unfortunately, Hayden can't join us for dinner. He has plans with his fiancée, Addison.

"Next time, though, for sure," he says.

In a totally teasing tone, since we're sure to have many opportunities to go out after games this season, I point at him as I back away. "I'm holding you to it, Harrington," I warn.

He just laughs and shoots me the middle finger.

Damn, I love these guys.

I have no siblings, so they really are like brothers to me.

And just like with real family, I'd do anything for them.

A short while later, Finn, Arden, and I are at an upscale steakhouse in downtown Atlanta, enjoying delicious filet mignon and lobster tail dinners.

The restaurant is all dark wood and Tudor trimming, accentuated by soft lighting. We're seated at a table in a back corner, affording us some much-appreciated privacy.

Though it isn't overly busy tonight, we've already received our fair share of stares and murmurs of "Wow, those guys play for the Thunder," especially as we were being led by the hostess back to our table.

But now there's no one around us.

That's how we like it. We can relax and be ourselves, which usually includes a lot of joking and teasing.

There's even some good-natured ribbing about Arden finally making amends for his flubbed goal in the playoffs.

Setting my fork down and wiping my mouth with a cloth napkin, I say to Arden, "Guess this means you'll be retiring your practice net and street balls, huh?"

Arden spent the early part of his summer practicing just about every imaginable shot out in his driveway, using his trusty practice net and numerous street balls. I know, as I was there to witness a few of those drills.

Dipping a piece of lobster meat into a small metal cup of warmed butter that's next to his plate, Arden scoffs. "Aw, fuck you, man. I put that net and those balls away months ago." Looking a little sheepish, he adds, "After I met Willow, I quit spending so much time making up for that fucked-up shot."

In a serious tone, I say quietly, "She really has been good for you, Arden."

"She has," he agrees as he pops the lobster into his mouth.

Finn chimes in, "Hey, speaking of Willow. How's it going with you two living together?"

Arden nods and swallows, then he says, "It's fantastic. I wouldn't want it any other way."

After taking a sip of water, I say, "Yeah, and now you'll have another person in the house—Ellie. So much for that lonely life you were once leading. Things sure have changed, man."

Sighing, Arden says, "True. A lot is different...and all for the better. But as for Ellie moving in, she's being her usual stubborn self."

Arden rolls his eyes, and Finn asks what I'm thinking, "How do you mean?"

I'm curious to hear his answer. I mean, if his sister isn't staying with him, where is she planning on living?

Shaking his head, Arden says, "Ellie told me she'll stay at my house a couple of days, but she won't live there. She claims she's not sure how long she'll be in Atlanta, but I'm thinking at least three months. Anyway, she doesn't want to be a 'third wheel' during that time." He rolls his eyes again. "Those are her words, not mine. I'd never think that, nor would Willow."

"Where's she going to stay, then?" I ask.

Leaning back, Arden says, "She's talking about living in an extended stay hotel. And honestly, I fucking hate that idea."

Hmmm, my house is in suburban Atlanta.

It's nice and roomy too.

And no one lives there but me.

My place is located at the end of a windy lane in a secluded neighborhood, but I'm still close to all of the conveniences, like shopping, restaurants, etc.

Before I can stop myself, I blurt out, "Your sister can stay with me, if she wants."

Arden's brow creases, like he's not sure why I'm offering for his sister to stay with me. I'm sure he's wondering if I have good intentions…or bad.

Nothing but good, I want to say.

But Finn is distracting me.

He's also looking over at me, but his expression is more one of confusion as to why I'm even throwing out an offer like this.

I don't know why myself.

I guess I just want to be nice.

Arden is such a good guy, and he really is my best friend. His sister shouldn't have to be stuck in a hotel somewhere.

Still, to make it clear that my intentions are nothing but pure, I amend, "I mean she can stay at my house, not *with* me. It's just…" I

15

sigh. "I have plenty of room. And we're on the road so much during the season. I won't even be around that much. And, Arden, you're like a damn brother to me. Both you dudes are. Hey, maybe Ellie can be the sister I never had."

Why do I have a sudden feeling that statement is going to bite me in the ass?

Shaking my head, I shrug it off.

Then I look around the table to see how what I just said is being received.

Okay, Arden looks relieved. He also looks like he's seriously considering taking me up on my offer.

But Finn is still peering over at me like I'm asking for trouble down the road.

Good God, what does he think?

That I'm going to make a move on Arden's little sister?

Or that I'm trying to set up a live-in hookup situation?

Neither is true. I'd never do anything like that.

Like I told Arden, his sister may as well be my sister.

So, rolling my eyes at Finn, I mutter under my breath, "Dude, come on."

He just puts his hands up and, making a *whatever* face, gets to work on cutting his steak.

Thankfully, Arden appears to be lost in thought. He's not even paying attention to us.

Looking over at him, I ask, "So, what do you think, Arden?"

Shrugging, he says, "I like the idea of Ellie staying somewhere safe. And with someone I know I can trust. Your house is probably the next best thing to her living at my place. Let me run it by her, though. It's her call at the end of the day."

I nod. "That's true. It is."

He releases a breath. "Okay, I'll ask Ellie and let you know what she says."

"Perfect," I reply, nodding.

I'm feeling good about helping out Arden and his sister, but, man, Finn is staring down at his plate and shaking his head, clearly trying not to laugh.

What does he know that I don't know?

Is Arden's sister like super hot or something?

Is she crazy gorgeous?

Even if she is, it's not like I'm some caveman.

I can control myself.

I'm sure she can too.

We'll simply be two adults sharing space, nothing more, nothing less.

Chapter

Three

ELLIE

I pull up to Arden's house a few minutes after midnight. When I left the sports bar, the rain had thankfully passed.

It was smooth sailing from that point on. I even made up for the time I lost by stopping for a break and a bite to eat.

And now I'm finally here.

Blowing out one long, relieved breath, I cut the engine and unbuckle my seat belt.

Time to go in.

But wait.

I hesitate. I don't want to just go up to the door and ring the doorbell. That would most likely wake up Willow. That's not good, as she has to be at work early tomorrow morning.

She told me as much the last time we talked. In fact, she was bummed she couldn't stay up and welcome me.

I'm sad, too, but I'll see her tomorrow.

I can't wait.

Willow and I, though we haven't met in person, get along really well. Once she and Arden were officially a couple, he introduced her to me on a Zoom call.

We hit it off and bonded right away. We actually talk a lot. Maybe that's because we're only a year apart. Plus, one of our favorite things to do is tease Arden about his age. He turned thirty this past spring, and we like to remind him all the time.

Good thing my brother has a good sense of humor.

Speaking of which, I'm ready to finally see him!

Smiling, I take my phone out of my purse and text Arden a simple *I'm here!*

I should have just done that from the start. He's probably anxiously awaiting my arrival.

Whoa, he is. He just busted out of the front door and is practically running down to my car.

Laughing, I pop open the driver-side door and jump out just as he rushes over to me.

Grabbing me up in a big, brotherly hug, he says, "Hey, Ellie. It's so fucking good to see you. I'm glad you're finally here."

Even though we text and FaceTime a lot, it's been a while since I've seen my brother in person.

That's why I hold onto him extra long.

Finally, I let go and step back.

Smiling, I tell him, "It has been too long. I missed you, big bro."

"I missed you too," he says. And then, raising a concerned brow, he asks, "How was the drive? Did you run into any rain?"

He knows my feelings on driving in the dreaded wet stuff.

Nodding, I say, "Yeah, but only once. A storm hit just outside Chattanooga. I stopped and waited it out."

"Good call," he says, nodding.

"Yeah, but..." I blow out a breath. "Besides that one incident, the ride down here has been pretty uneventful."

"Good, good." Pointing back to the trunk, he asks, "Is your suitcase in there? I can carry it up to the house for you."

I break into a grin. "Suitcases, you mean, plural. And yes, they're in the trunk."

Using the key fob, I pop it open.

Chuckling, Arden heads to the back of the car, where he easily lifts out my bags.

Though they're both oversized and packed to their limits, I still have to sigh and say, "Pretty sad that my whole life fits into two suitcases, huh?"

Arden pshaws. "Oh, stop, Ellie. You have stuff back at Mom and Dad's house. This isn't all you own."

He's right, but my life in Chicago, brief though it was, does indeed fit into two bags. There's no denying that.

But now is not the time to dwell on the past. I'm here to start a new chapter, one where I plan to have a little fun before I decide exactly what I want to do next with my life.

As my brother and I head into his house, I share with him that I was able to catch some of his game.

I, of course, don't mention how I was lusting hard over Nils while I sat and ate my burger and fries, wondering all the while what *he* tastes like.

Yeah, I don't think Arden would want to hear about that.

Nor would he approve.

So I focus instead on when the game went into overtime.

"Hey," I say, nudging him with my elbow. "That was a great goal there at the end. Way to go."

Setting my suitcases down in the entry hall, and looking quite pleased with himself, as he should, he replies, "Thanks, Ellie."

Softly, I say, "I know how much it meant for you to get the winning goal against that team."

My brother took it so hard that he flubbed a shot, one that could have won the Thunder their playoff game and the series that round.

I'm happy when his blue eyes meet my turquoise ones and he says, "Yeah, I can now truly and completely put that loss behind me."

I know he means it.

Arden told me how Willow played a big part in him moving on from that missed shot, but I know my brother, and I'm certain he felt he needed to prove something to his teammates.

Namely, that that bad chapter is behind them all.

It is—it's a new season.

Really, it's a new season for all of us.

Arden yawns, and I'm reminded of how late it is.

Shit, I'm tired too.

"Hey," I begin, "let's get some sleep. We can catch up more tomorrow."

"Yeah, sounds good," Arden mumbles as he stifles another yawn. As he picks up my suitcases, he says, "Follow me, Ellie. Willow and I made up a bedroom for you just down the hall here on the first floor. Ours is upstairs, so we were thinking this way you'll have your own bathroom and some privacy."

Uh-oh, does he think I'm staying at his house long term?

As I follow him down a darkened hall, I remind him, "I'm only going to be here a few days, Arden. Just until I find a decent extended stay hotel that I like. I checked out a few online, but I'd prefer to see them in person before I make a decision."

I hear him huff as we reach what will be my room…for now.

As he steps inside, he hits a switch that turns on a small lamp on a nightstand next to a full-size bed.

I look around.

The bedroom is nice, decorated in neutral sand and brown tones.

Arden sets my suitcases down on the floor and turns to me. "Yeah," he says, "about that extended stay hotel idea…"

As he trails off, I state firmly, "Hey, I'm not budging on not living here. I am just not going to impede on your relationship with Willow. It's too fresh and too new. I mean, shit, you guys just moved in together. So yeah, no"—I shake my head—"there's nothing you can say to change my mind about living somewhere else."

There really isn't, and he knows it. He and Willow should have this time to themselves. My staying here in their space would kind of be like me coming along on their honeymoon.

Eww, no.

Holding up his hands in placation, my brother says, "No, I'm not going to try to change your mind. I know you're set on not living with us, and I respect that decision. But what if I told you there may be another place, besides a hotel, where you can stay?"

Hmm, this is an interesting turn of events.

Intrigued, I cross my arms and say, "And just where would that be?"

Slowly, like he wants to parse out the details to ease me into the idea, he says, "You could stay at a teammate's house. One who lives alone, and has a huge place. I think it would work out well. We have plenty of road games, as you know, so you'd have the whole house to yourself a lot of the time. Even when he's there, this guy is someone I can completely trust."

Hearing that last part, I scoff. "Someone you can completely trust? What does that even mean, Arden? Do you think I don't have a mind of my own?"

He levels me with a stern look. "Ellie, you know I don't mean it that way. I'm just saying that, capable as you are, it makes me more comfortable knowing you wouldn't have to ward off any unwanted advances. This guy is truly trustworthy."

Rolling my eyes, I relent. "Okay, okay. I see your point. So who is this 'truly trustworthy' teammate you want me to be roomies with?"

I'm imagining it's one of the few not very attractive guys on the team. I can see Arden thinking I'd not be tempted if the dude's an ogre.

I'm mildly irritated still.

But then I just about pass out when Arden says, "The teammate I'm talking about is Nils Sten."

Holy crap!

What?

This could not be any more perfect if I had scripted it. The guy I have my eyes set on, and Arden is serving him up to me on a silver platter.

Hell, yeah!

But I have to play it cool.

If he catches on that I'm in any way attracted to Nils, he'll call this whole thing off. Arden will be all on board the extended hotel-train, then.

Fuck that.

I'm staying with Nils.

Making a face like I'm deeply contemplating this proposal and not really sure how I feel about it, I say, "Oh, I don't know. I'd hate to ask that of him."

"You don't have to ask," Arden says. "Nils actually offered."

"He did?" I blurt out, stunned. "Why would he do such a thing?"

Arden sighs. "He's just a good guy like that, Ellie. And we're very good friends. In fact, he said something that was pretty funny, but may actually happen."

"Oh, yeah," I say, curious. "What's that?"

"He said you'll probably end up being like the sister he never had."

What?

Good God, we don't want that!

Of course, I can't say any of this to Arden.

So, smiling slyly, I just murmur, "Mmm, yeah, maybe. You never know."

Yeah, right.

"So, what do you think?" he asks. "Do you want to stay with Nils?"

Do I ever!

I need to still play it like I'm not sure, so I hedge, "I don't know, Arden. I guess if you're absolutely sure he's okay with it, I'll consider it."

He assures me, "He is definitely more than okay with it."

I shrug. "Then okay. Sure. I guess I am too."

Internally, I'm cheering—*Yes!*

Arden looks pleased, as well, but for a completely different reason.

"That's great," he says, smiling. "I feel better already knowing you'll be living at Nils's house. We can work out the logistics later, but I'll let him know you said 'yes' to staying at his place."

"All right." I nod.

We wrap up, and Arden leaves me alone in my temporary bedroom.

I sit down on the edge of the bed and start smiling like crazy.

I cannot believe I am going to be freaking living at Nils's house.

I can put my fun little plan to seduce him into effect immediately.

Or maybe, if I end up really liking him as a person, there could be more.

It's a possibility, right?

Since I'll have him all to myself quite a bit, I could potentially get him to fall for me—like head over heels in love.

Okay, I know I'm getting way ahead of myself.

But still, wouldn't that be something?

Chapter

Four

NILS

"**D**ude, what is your fucking problem?"

We just finished up with our afternoon practice, and Finn and I are walking to our cars. Arden parked in a different area of the players' lot, so we already parted ways with him.

Good. Now that I'm alone with Finn I finally have a chance to get to the bottom of why he finds it so amusing that Ellie agreed to move into my house.

That's right, she did. And when, in the locker room before we hit the ice, Arden told me she was up for staying with me, Finn let out a snort that even had Arden looking over at him curiously.

He didn't question him about his strange reaction, though.

But I sure the fuck am, right now.

"Seriously," I go on, "you were weird last night at the restaurant when I threw out the idea of Arden's sister staying with me. And now today in the locker room—that snort? What the fuck is up with you?"

Finn stops at his graphite-gray Cadillac Escalade, which is parked next to my black Range Rover.

As we both open the back hatches of our respective vehicles and load in our sticks and bags, he says, "It's just…" He pauses what he's doing and looks over at me. "Have you ever *seen* Arden's sister?"

Placing my last stick in the back cargo area of my vehicle and closing the hatch, I cross my arms and reply, "No, I haven't. Why are you asking?"

He closes his back door and turns to face me. "Dude, she's fucking beautiful. Like, I don't know how you're *not* going to be attracted to her. And that thing about her being the sister you never had?" He chuffs, "Never going to happen, my friend. Never."

Okay, now I'm curious, so I ask, "First off, how do you even know what she looks like? It's not like she's in the public eye. I mean, she's been away at college for four years. When did you even have a chance to meet her? I don't recall her ever coming to any games."

"I haven't met her," Finn replies. "But one day a while ago, Arden and I were talking about family. He showed me some pictures on his phone. A couple of them were of Ellie, and, man, I'm telling you…" His eyes hold mine meaningfully. "She is fucking hot. Think long raven-black hair, turquoise eyes, big boobs, and a tight little bod. Shit, dude…" He shakes his head and chuckles. "You are in for it. This will truly be a test of your friendship with Arden."

Bristling, I uncross my arms. "Now wait just a minute. What do you think I am? Some maniac who has no self-control? We have beautiful women throwing themselves at us all of the time, and it's not like I'm out there bedding each and every one."

"Yeah, but there have been a few you couldn't resist," he reminds me with a sly look.

I volley back, "Ah, hell, same for you, dude."

He holds up his hands. "I know, I know. I'm guilty as charged. I think we've all been there once or twice. Some guys even more."

On that, he's right. Every single one of us has had our moments of weakness, or sometimes we just felt like being bad boys. But most of my antics are in the past. Now that I'm twenty-seven, I've calmed down a lot.

And that's why, gorgeous or not, I'm sure I can not look at Arden's sister in any way other than her being my own damn relative.

I tell Finn I won't be tempted, and he laughs. "I don't know, man. All I'm saying is good luck with that."

I roll my eyes at him.

Ignoring me, he asks, "So, when is she moving in?"

"Tonight. Since we have a three-game road trip coming up, Arden and I figured we should get her settled into my place before we leave town. This way she can have the house to herself a little while before I return. Hopefully, that'll give her a chance to get comfortable without me hovering around."

As Finn takes a step backward along the side of his SUV, readying to leave, he points at me with his key fob and chuckles. "Hovering around is a good way to put it. Because that's what you're going to want to do once you get back."

I pshaw. "Aw, fuck you, Finn. I'm going to prove you so wrong."

Stopping, he raises a brow and asks, "Want to make a wager on that?"

We like to bet on shit all the time, so I nod and say, "Sure. Let's do it."

"Okay, so..." He thinks about it, then says, "If you sleep with Ellie, then for two weeks you have to do all of my dirty laundry. And I mean all of it. No sending it out, no getting someone else to do it."

I snort. "Ugh, that's disgusting. And fuck that. You're talking small potatoes. Let's make this bet bigger and better than that."

"All right, okay." His eyes dart to my beauty—my Range Rover. Tapping the side panel, he says, "If you lose, then I get the title to this baby."

I gasp, "Not my Rover, dude. I ordered it customized to my exact specifications. Hell, it took fucking forever for it to come in."

Scoffing, Finn says tauntingly, "You're that sure you're going to lose, huh?"

Aw, hell, I can win this.

I am not *ever* sleeping with Arden's sister.

And because I plan to be victorious, I up the ante. "Okay, agreed. And if you lose, then I get your Escalade."

He nods thoughtfully before proclaiming with a level of self-confidence that's downright worrisome, "You've got yourself a deal, my friend."

We shake on it, before we hop into the two vehicles now in play and up for grabs.

Hands on the steering wheel, but before I put the Rover into Reverse, a feeling of dread washes over me.

What if I lose?

Shit.

I let out a snort.

No, I'm not worried. I know I'll win. Not only do I have impeccable self-control, but there's no way I'm giving up my prized Range Rover.

Yeah, I got this.

Chapter

Five

ELLIE

Willow arrives home from work before Arden gets back from his afternoon practice. The guys are leaving for a three-game road stint tomorrow, so my brother and I agreed that it'd be best for me to move into Nils's house before they head out.

I'm pumped to get over there, but I'm also a little sad that I won't have more time to hang out with Willow. She's so nice, and we get along just as well in person as we did over the phone.

To my surprise and delight, since I'm starving, she brought home delicious—and huge—grilled chicken salads.

There's one for Arden for when he gets home, but she and I just couldn't wait to dig in.

We're seated in the kitchen now, chowing down.

"How's this going to work tonight?" she asks. "Are you going to follow Arden over to Nils's house?"

"Yeah," I reply as I spear a lettuce leaf along with a piece of chicken. "Originally, I was just going to put Nils's address in the GPS and drive over myself, but Arden wants to make official introductions and all that." Raising the fork to my mouth, I laugh. "You know how he is."

Nodding, her strawberry blonde curls bouncing, she says, "Oh, I know. That sounds very Arden-like." She takes a small bite of her salad, and once she swallows, she sets her fork down. Sighing, she goes on, "I wish I could go with you guys, but we're really backed up with our end-of-third-quarter reports. Much as I don't want to, I'm going to have to stay here at the house and do some work on the computer."

Willow is an accountant for the Thunder organization, and at this time of the year, with the season starting and the financial third quarter ending, work has been really hectic for her.

"Aw, I understand," I reply, waving my fork. "But once things settle down, we'll have to do something just the two of us."

"For sure," she agrees. "I bet we can find some kind of trouble to get into."

I laugh, as she's probably right.

That makes me even more certain that not living here at their house is definitely the right call. Not only do I now get to stay with Nils—*yes!*—where I can work on my secret plan to seduce him, but also, if I were living here, I'd definitely want to hang out with Willow a lot.

I doubt Arden would love that. Sure, he'd be cool about it at first, but it just wouldn't be good long term. Like I told him from the start, he and Willow need time alone to fully bond and grow as a couple.

I truly believe that.

And I want them to work.

Having Willow as my sister-in-law someday would be amazing.

I hope Arden marries her.

Yeesh, now that I don't have school and work to occupy my mind, it seems thoughts of romance are filling in the gaps.

Well, I can get into that, starting with my own romantic endeavors getting underway.

I chuckle to myself, as once I put my plan into action, Nils isn't going to know what hit him.

Chapter

Six

NILS

Shit, man, I am in trouble. Fucking Finn wasn't kidding—Arden's sister, Ellie, is drop-dead gorgeous.

From the moment she pulled up in my driveway, behind Arden, and stepped out of her silver Jaguar, I've been picking my jaw up off the ground.

I knew I shouldn't have come outside to meet them. Everything Finn told me about Ellie is true. From the way the setting sun is making her raven-black hair, tumbling down her back in a cascade of soft curls, look so damn shiny and soft, to how her short-ass jean shorts show off her tan legs to perfection, I have a feeling I'm done for.

And the assault is relentless.

When I glance up from her legs, my eyes are drawn to how her white blouse is unbuttoned just enough to afford me a glimpse of her ample cleavage.

My dick takes note of that.

And now Arden, who thankfully appears to be blissfully unaware that his sister has me under her captive spell, introduces us.

As we stand in the driveway next to her car, he waves his hand between the two of us and says, "Nils, this is Ellie. Ellie, Nils."

"Nice to meet you," I say with a nod.

God, her eyes really are fucking turquoise.

"You too," she replies softly, extending her hand.

Wow, I even like her voice.

We shake, and her skin is so soft and warm.

I quickly pull away, and I swear she looks…smug?

Okay, I clearly need to get it together. I, Nils Sten, am not some lapdog. And this isn't like me anyway. I'm not so easily captivated by any woman.

Clearing my throat, I motion to the brick walkway leading up to the front door of my home and say, "Are you ready to go in, Ellie? I can show you around. Oh, and we can put your bags in your new bedroom. I'm giving you one with an en suite bathroom. It's the next biggest to the master, which is mine, so it's pretty nice."

That's a lot of detail, dude. Quit acting like a high schooler mesmerized by the homecoming queen. You don't need to impress her.

Luckily for me, Ellie doesn't seem fazed. She just nods and replies, "Sounds nice. Thanks. Let's go check it out."

Before we head inside, Arden and I take out Ellie's two large suitcases from the trunk of her car.

He mentions to me that he'd like to get back home to spend some time with Willow before we go on the road tomorrow, adding, "Ellie is okay with me taking off, so if you don't mind…"

I stop him there. "Not a problem, man. I got it from here."

And I do.

So, while Arden and Ellie hug and say goodbye, I take the bags up to the house. I place her suitcases just inside the door, then step back outside to wait for her.

Ellie waves to Arden as he drives off, then makes her way up to the front entryway.

I try not to watch her, as I'm turning into a total creeper here.

This has to stop.

Stepping aside and motioning with my hand, I smile and say, "Ladies first."

"My, aren't you just the gentleman," she replies with a soft laugh as she steps past me and into the entry hall.

Little flirt.

This does not help me behave. I shouldn't like her flirting. But I do.

Ellie seems fun.

And I love fun.

Speaking of love, I absolutely love the way her ass looks in her shorts as I follow her in.

Yeah, I'm totally checking her out again.

I'm glad when she turns around to face me, simply because it gets me back in-line.

Adopting a serious tone, though I bet it'll be short-lived, Ellie says, "Hey, before we go on, I just want to say thank you so much for letting me stay here. I promise not to be too much of a bother. And if I am, just let me know. Also, I know you told Arden you don't want any rent, but I can certainly help out with things like cleaning and stuff."

I wave my hand. "Ellie, yes, you're right on the no-rent thing. But you don't have to clean. I have a housekeeper who comes in once a week on Fridays. Just make yourself at home. Besides, you're kind of doing me a favor by staying here."

"I am?" She looks surprised. "How so?"

"Well…" I blow out a breath. "I'll be gone a lot for away games, and I think it'll be a nice change to have someone around when I come home."

Cocking her head and bedazzling me with a million-dollar smile, she says, "Well, I promise I'll try to be good company, then."

Oh, I am in so much trouble.

Good thing I'll be on the road often.

Picking up her bags and shaking my head, I murmur, "Don't worry. You already are."

After I show Ellie the bedroom that'll be hers for her stay, one that happens to be right down the hall from mine—*help me! What was I thinking?*—I give her a tour of the whole house. I also hand her a key and fill her in on the code to the alarm. Finally, we exchange cell phone numbers in case she needs to reach me, or I have to talk to her.

This all occurs in the entertainment room, our final stop on my tour, while we're standing next to a plushy leather sofa facing the massive big-screen TV on the wall.

Now that the tour is over, though, I'm not sure what to do next.

I'd like to make Ellie feel comfortable, and I don't think running off and leaving her alone would result in that. Not to mention, I actually want to spend time with her. I'd like to start getting to know her as a person. It'd be nice if we became friends.

So, turning to her, I say, "I think it's only like seven or something. Would you want to stay in here and watch a movie? We can order food if you're hungry."

I'm much more composed now than I was earlier.

I haven't even been checking her out.

Well, okay, I have, but not nearly as much as before.

See, I can do this.

Finn will not win our bet.

And Arden won't have to kill me.

I am a good, trustworthy dude. One you can definitely allow to house your hot-as-fuck sister and not worry he'll try to bed her.

Nope, not me.

I'm so wrapped up in pumping myself up that I totally miss her reply.

"I'm sorry. What was that?"

Chuckling, she says, "I said sure. I'm up for a movie."

"And food?"

She shakes her head. "No, I'm good. I had a huge salad earlier with Willow, so I'm still pretty full. But if you're hungry, don't let me stop you from getting something."

"No." I shake my head once. "I'm actually fine too."

After we sit down on the sofa, I turn on the TV. We check out all of the options on my many streaming services, and ultimately decide to watch something scary.

Our selection is a new slasher flick with a B-level cast. Sometimes those are the best. But even if it's not that great, a horror movie feels fitting and timely, seeing as it is October, and Halloween is coming up in a few weeks.

There is one other reason I prefer the scary movie choice. I sure as fuck don't want to watch any kind of romantic movie with Ellie.

Or, God forbid, anything with sex scenes.

Hell, no.

Bring on the slasher flick.

Before I start the movie, Ellie slides over to the other end of the sofa and tucks her legs up under her.

I scoot down away from her to the far side.

We watch the movie, and it turns out to be just okay. Certainly not an Oscar contender or anything, but there are a few good scares. The film keeps my attention enough that I only sneak in a few surreptitious glances over at Ellie.

So, all in all, I behave.

I'm feeling more comfortable, so after the movie is over, I turn off the TV and, twisting on the sofa to face her, I ask Ellie, "What did you think? Did you like it?"

Sweeping her long dark hair over one shoulder and twirling a strand around her index finger, she says, "It was decent. I was surprised a few times."

"Yeah," I tease, "I thought I saw you over there jumping once or twice."

"*Riiight.*" She rolls her eyes at me. "I think that was you doing the jumping, not me."

Rolling back my shoulders and puffing up my chest, I declare, "No way. I don't scare that easily."

She snorts. "Okay, tough guy. Whatever you say."

We look over at each other, and, as our eyes meet, we both bust out laughing.

This is good; we're already joking around and acting like goofy siblings.

See, I knew I could be strong.

Now all I have to do is not think about, or lust over, her luscious legs…or her hot ass…or her beautiful eyes…or her pretty face…or anything else.

And if I do all those things, I'll be driving around in Finn's Escalade in no time, victorious and safe from Arden's wrath.

Chapter

Seven

ELLIE

As I lie in another new bed in what will be my room for a while, I think about what a genuinely good time I had tonight watching a scary movie with Nils.

I liked it even better afterward when we talked and joked around a bit.

All in all, I can definitely say I like Nils.

And not just because he's hot.

He's a cool person.

Nils is funny, kind of a smartass, laid-back, and nice. He's clearly a good guy, just like Arden said he was.

I can see why they're such good friends.

But one thing Arden never mentioned—not that he ever would— is that Nils is *waaay* hotter in person. It was all I could do to play it cool when I first met him outside in his driveway.

His green eyes really are the color of freaking emeralds, and his messy dark blond hair looks so silky and soft.

He had on a tight dark olive tee that showed off his corded forearms, huge biceps, and wide chest. And don't think I didn't notice how big his quads looked in the ripped, faded jeans he had on.

Damn, I'd really like to climb that man like a tree.

And do a lot of sinful things to him.

I sigh.

There will be time for that.

I hope.

For now, I was happy just watching a movie with him. Not only did it allow us to start to get to know each other and bond a little, but it gave me many opportunities to slyly glance over at his yummy body and drool.

Not literally, but in my mind.

He is so sexy.

Clearly my crush on him has gone nuclear.

I really fucking want that man.

And not just as a fling.

That's right, I've decided already that I want more. I knew this could happen after I met him. And it has. My change of heart to escalate my plan from a hookup to potentially more was never out of the realm of possibility. My crush on this man has always been huge.

Only thing is this means my plan to bed Nils just got a whole lot more complicated.

That's okay. I have nothing but time—time to not only get him to want me but time to allow him to fall for me.

We're off to a promising start.

I made some headway when we first met out in the driveway. He was totally checking me out. He thought he was being sly, but I caught him on more than one occasion.

I guess my flirting worked. The skimpy jean shorts and low-buttoned blouse I chose to wear didn't hurt my cause, either.

In fact, my outfit was still working its magic down in the entertainment room. With the way I had my legs curled up under me, which was totally by design, they were on full display.

I saw Nils glancing over at me several times, but more so when we were watching the first half of the movie. Either he had steeled himself or he was really immersed in that stupid flick.

Hmm, I think the former is correct.

Well, if he did steel himself, I'll be working on that.

I'll get his attention again.

I have a few days to think of some ways to do so, seeing as Nils will be away starting tomorrow.

Oooh, but when that man gets back, he'd better watch out.

'Cause this is so fucking on!

The next morning, after I take a shower and throw on black leggings and a navy blue blouse, I pad down to the kitchen to find something to eat.

I discover the fridge and pantry are well stocked with lots of options, but I opt for just cereal and a glass of orange juice.

Sitting down at the table, I fill the bowl with cereal, then milk, all the while thinking, *Man, the house sure is quiet.*

Nils is gone, as I knew he'd be. He told me last night, before we parted ways in the upstairs hallway next to my bedroom, that the team was flying out early this morning.

I replied, "Well, have a good trip and win all of your games. I'll see you when you get back."

Chuckling, he said, "Yeah, thanks. We'll try." He then shifted from one foot to the other as he ran his fingers through his sexy, mussed-up hair. Hair that I'd like to run *my* fingers through. After a pause, he cocked his head and with his emerald eyes meeting mine, he added, "Maybe we can have another movie night when I get back."

Inside, I was all like *Yes!*

But I kept myself composed as I said, calmly and in an even tone, "Sure, that'd be fun."

"Great." He turned to leave. "Then I guess I'll see you in a few days. Good night, Ellie."

I popped open the door to my room and murmured, "'Night, Nils."

Is it crazy that I can't wait to see him again?

Unfortunately, I have a few days to wait.

And I better get used to it.

It's going to be like this the whole time I'm here.

That gets me to thinking that having a plan to make Nils mine is not enough. I need something more to do, something productive, something to keep me busy.

Dipping my spoon into my cereal, I say out loud, "I need a job."

Yeah, that'd be perfect. I can bring in some money and contribute, as well, without dipping into my savings. Despite what Nils said, I plan to help out in some way to repay his kindness. Buying groceries and cooking a few meals would be a good start.

As I eat my breakfast, I think about my job options.

I bet I can get back on with Applebee's pretty easily. I made good tips this summer. And wouldn't you know it; I even packed my "uniform"—black pants and a black polo-style shirt with their logo—in case I did decide to go this route.

I'm sure there's an Applebee's close by, right?

I mean, they're all over the country.

I check my phone and discover there's one only five miles away.

Perfect—looks like I know exactly where I'll be going today.

Chapter

Eight

NILS

wonder how Ellie is doing back in Atlanta. I hate to admit it, but she's been on my mind a lot.

And she's certainly starred in a few of my fantasies.

I could always text her, but that might be weird. I have no real reason to, and when we exchanged phone numbers, it was only in case one of us really needed to reach the other.

It wasn't for the purpose of checking in.

Though we had a pleasant-enough evening watching the movie, we're not yet friends or anything.

So yeah, it'd be really strange for me to text her.

That's why I won't.

But I really *want* to.

Shit, this has got to stop.

Not just because I shouldn't be thinking this way, but more so due to the fact that my line is about to hit the ice.

Yeah, I'm in the middle of a game!

It's the final leg of our three-game road trip, and we're playing the Boston Bruins.

We won one of our previous matchups and lost the other.

This game, though, is looking promising. We're up 4–2 midway through the third period. One more goal would be good insurance.

So let's do this.

I fly off the bench and over the boards with my linemates, Arden and Hayden. Our more stay-at-home defenseman shoots the puck into the Bruins' zone. All of us start chasing after it, but Arden gets to it first.

So does a Bruin, however, so now he and Arden are battling for the puck in the corner.

Though I have a guy covering me pretty well, I somehow manage to position myself in front of the Bruins' net.

My opponent tries to bump me away, but I'm strong on my skates and hold steady.

Arden comes up with the puck and passes it to me. Though that defenseman is all over my ass, I manage to get off a clean shot.

And…I score!

We're up 5–2 now, and there are only about eight minutes left in the period. Still, anything can happen, so our coach has us tighten up to a much more defensive style of play.

The strategy works, and we win the game.

Two out of three road game wins is respectable. We earned four out of six possible points.

Not bad.

It's been a good run, but I'm ready to go home.

When I leave the arena with Arden and Finn, we stop out on the sidewalk to decide whether to go back to the hotel our team is staying in or grab a bite to eat.

Since the crisp New England autumn air is really whipping around us, I pull the collar of the long trench coat I have on over my suit up and around the sides of my neck.

There, that's better.

Jerking my chin to an Italian restaurant that's right across the street, I say, "I'm fucking starving, so I vote for food."

Finn is in total agreement, but Arden tells us, "Actually, you guys go ahead. I think I'm going to head back to the hotel and turn in."

"Okay, old man," I tease.

We all love poking fun at Arden since he turned thirty. In actuality, though, I know he wants to go back to his room and FaceTime with Willow. It's been several days now that we've been on the road, so I'm sure he's missing her.

Kind of like how I'm missing Ellie.

Okay, it's not quite the same, as my longing to get back and see Ellie is more about wanting to get to know her better.

Only as a friend, of course.

That's what I keep telling myself, anyway.

Finn laughs and says something else about Arden getting old.

Our friend snorts. "Ah, fuck off, you two. You're right behind me. Only three more years and you'll both be thirty as well."

"Shit, he has a point," Finn says.

Chuckling, I reply, "Great. We can all ship off to the retirement home together."

Arden, playing along, starts to back away.

Pointing at us, he says, "Just know I play a mean game of bingo, boys. Better brush up on your skills."

I snort. "Fuck bingo. We'll be playing cards, like we do on the team plane."

Finn, his expression turning serious, says, "Now, wait just a minute. Can we bet on bingo? If so, let's not rule it out."

Laughing and turning away, Arden waves goodbye and throws out over his shoulder, "Finn, you can bet on anything in this life. Haven't you figured that out by now?"

Shit, he's right.

If he only knew that Finn and I have a current wager on his baby sister.

Yeah, I think we'll keep that one to ourselves.

As Arden turns a corner and walks out of view, Finn and I cross over to the restaurant.

This is the first I've had any real alone time with him. It always seems like someone is around, usually Arden. I sure as hell can't express my real thoughts on Ellie in front of him.

But I can to Finn.

So, as we reach the entrance of the restaurant, I stop and say, "By the way, speaking of bets and all that, you weren't fucking kidding about Arden's sister."

Laughing, he says, "She's beautiful, right?"

I nod. "Stunning."

"And that body?" he asks, raising a brow.

"Exquisite."

"Told you so," he gloats.

What can I say?

He sure the fuck did.

But that doesn't mean I'm losing the wager.

I tell him as much, and he says, "We'll see about that. I think you'd better get that Range Rover detailed and ready for me."

I chortle, "You wish. You'll be eating your words when I'm cruising around in your Escalade."

That makes him laugh. "You're delusional, man." Opening the restaurant door, he says, "Time will tell, but until then, let's fucking eat."

I can't argue with that.

We head into what turns out to be an old-style Italian eatery. I like it—the place has charm. It's not all that busy, which is great, but we still ask for a seat in the back.

The hostess leads us to a nice private booth in a far-away corner. We take off our coats and sit down across from each other.

After a beat, a waiter comes over with menus and two glasses of ice water.

We thank him as he hands us the menus and places the waters on the table.

After he leaves, we peruse our options.

"What are you thinking about getting?" I ask Finn.

"Hmm, let me see." He taps the menu. "This Delmonico steak with a side of pasta sounds good."

"It does," I agree. "In fact, I think that's what I'm getting."

"Yeah, me too," he says with finality.

When the waiter returns, we both order the steak and pasta.

Once he's out of sight, Finn asks me how the first night with Ellie went.

Chuckling, he says, "You didn't hook up with her and lose our bet already, did you? You could just be holding out on me."

"Yeah, right, dickhead." I roll my eyes at him. "No, nothing like that happened. Not even close. Our night was purely platonic. We watched a movie and then sat and chilled for a while."

He nods. "Sounds nice. And hey, by the way, I'm just giving you a hard time. I know nothing happened. You have more willpower than to lose our bet on the first night."

"Gee, thanks," I mutter.

Ignoring my sarcasm, he asks, "So, is Ellie cool? I'm guessing if she's anything like Arden, she's pretty awesome."

Our dinner salads arrive, so we wait until the waiter leaves again to continue our conversation.

When he's out of earshot, I plunge my fork into my salad and nod. "Yeah, she's great. She's easy to be around. We hit it off right away."

"Any flirting?" he asks.

I have to be honest, so, after I finish my bite of salad, I share, "Yeah, she's a fucking huge flirt. But I think that's just who she is. She likes to joke around a lot too."

"Just who she is, huh?" Finn asks. He takes a sip of water, looking doubtful. Setting his glass down, he says, "Maybe she's attracted to you, Nils. And that's why she was flirting."

Uh-oh, what if he's right?

'Cause God knows I'm attracted to her.

Since I don't even want to entertain the implications of us both being attracted to each other, I shake my head and insist, "Nah, like I said, it's just who she is."

Finn snorts, then says, "Okay, so I have an idea."

"Uh-oh, what?"

I'm leery, as you never know what this guy might come up with.

Sure enough, he says, "Maybe when we have an opportunity, we should put it to a test. If Ellie flirts with me, then we'll know that's just how she is with everybody. But if not…" He cocks his head and raises a brow that says more than words ever could.

Great. Just great.

But since I know I'm right—I hope—I stab a tomato wedge with more force than necessary and say, "Yeah, sure. When you finally meet her, we'll see how she is with you."

Ugh.

I don't like this.

Why does the thought of Ellie flirting with Finn bother me so much?

It shouldn't, not at all, but it does.

So, what does that say about me and how I feel about her?

Nothing I care to think about right now.

Chapter

Nine

ELLIE

Autumn in the south sure is different from autumn in the north. While the leaves on the trees in Chicago are surely in full color change right about now, some probably even falling off, here in Atlanta there's just the slightest hint of yellow and splashes of orange.

And the weather?

Don't even get me started.

It's so sunny and warm out today that it's to the point of being almost downright hot.

No, check that—it *is* hot.

That's why I've chosen a light flouncy floral sundress and sandals to wear for my job hunt.

Not that it's much of a "hunt." I'm only trying Applebee's. In fact, I'm on my way there now. Hopefully, they'll have an opening for a server.

Then again, isn't everyone looking for employees these days?

I should be good.

When I reach Applebee's, I pull into their lot and park in a space on the side of the restaurant.

As I'm walking in, I see that, sure enough, there's a big "Now Hiring" sign on the door.

Cool. With my experience working at one of their Chicago locations over the summer, I should get hired today.

Once I'm inside, I ask the hostess if I can see the manager. I explain that I'm looking for a job and that I worked at an Applebee's recently.

She turns to head to the back, tossing over her shoulder, "Just one minute. I'll see if our manager is busy."

"Okay."

As I wait, I shift from one foot to the other. But I'm not waiting long. The manager, an older lady, her dark hair pulled up in a tight bun with graying at her temples, comes out to greet me so quickly, it's not even funny.

"Hi." She extends her hand, and says warmly, "I'm Barb. I hear you're interested in becoming a server here at Applebee's and that you have experience at one of our restaurants in the Chicago area?"

"Yes, I am." I shake her hand. "And I do have experience. Oh, by the way, I'm Ellie."

"Nice to meet you, Ellie." She motions for me to follow her. "Let's sit down in a booth, and we can talk further."

"Great."

I follow her to a booth just a few feet away. We sit down across from each other.

Glancing around, I note that it's not very busy, even though it's only a little after one. There should be a much larger lunch crowd.

The lack of customers gives me pause and makes me worry how

many tips I could really make here.

Hmmm...

But I put my concerns behind me, as I need a job.

The interview goes well, and Barb hires me on the spot.

As I'm leaving, an employee, clearly finishing her shift based on her black pants and regulation black polo, follows me. She's juggling her purse and a large cloth tote, which is slipping from her hand, so I hold the door for her.

"Thanks," she says as she readjusts her bags, one over each shoulder.

I smile. "No worries."

The girl is pretty. She has auburn hair, pulled up in a high ponytail, green eyes, and a smattering of freckles across her nose.

I start to walk to my car, and she continues to follow me, explaining that she's parked on the same side as me.

"I'm not a creeper, I promise," she says.

I just laugh.

I get the sense she has something she wants to tell me, but I have no clue what that could be.

Is the restaurant closing permanently or something along those lines? Could be, since it isn't that busy during a time when it should be bustling.

Well, it's not something I'm going to worry about now.

Just as I'm about to jump into my car, the girl stops and says, "Hey, can I ask you a question?"

With my hand on the top of my open door, I say, "Yeah, sure."

She walks over to where I'm standing and asks, "Are you planning on working here?"

"Uh-huh." I nod. "Barb, your manager, just hired me."

She smiles. "Aw, Barb is a sweetheart. But I should warn you, it's pretty slow most of the time. I mean, we get some business, sure. But tips really aren't what they should be."

"Ugh." I blow out a frustrated breath. "I was afraid of that. I guess I could try some other restaurants." I glance around the busy business area. "There seems to be a lot of options around here."

"There are." She hesitates, then asks, "Is it okay if I suggest one in particular?"

I'm not sure where this is going, or why she's being so helpful, but I shrug and say, "Sure."

Before she gives me her "suggestion," she says, "I'm Sammie, by the way."

"Oh, I'm Ellie. Nice to meet you."

"You too. So, anyway…" She releases a breath. "I swear I'm not a weirdo or anything, like I said before. But the fact is you're really pretty, and I know a place where you can make five times the tips you'll make here. Probably more than that even. I work there myself." She lifts the tote strap off her shoulder an inch or so and says, "That's what's in here—my other uniform. I'm heading there next."

I'm really curious, so I cross my arms and say, "Okay, I'm listening. What is this fabulous place with the great tips?"

Straightening the tote on her shoulder, she says, "Well, first, have you ever heard of Tilted Kilt or Hooters?"

"Yep." I nod. "I've heard of both of them."

She goes on. "Good. So, the place I'm talking about is not one of those, but it's a lot like them. The food is a little more upscale, but anyway." She waves her hand. "It's still a waitressing gig, like here at Applebee's, but the outfit you wear is kind of skimpy." I frown, and she quickly adds, "It's nothing too revealing, okay? You'd be wearing a white button-down blouse tied at the waist, a short red-and-black plaid skirt with black boy shorts underneath, and high leather boots with heels. I mean, I don't want to scare you away."

"Don't worry," I assure her, chuckling. "I'm not scared. I'm actually intrigued. Tell me more."

Nodding and looking relieved, she says, "Okay, the cool thing is, it's not a corporate bar or restaurant. It's privately owned. You get a nice hourly wage, better than here or at those other places I mentioned. And the tips on top of the wages are fantastic. Mostly guys come in, and they're big spenders."

I laugh. "Hmm, I wonder why."

Chuckling, she replies, "Right. But I have to say they're truly good tippers." She points to the southbound side of the busy four-lane road to the left of us. "It's about half a mile down from here. It's called Boots."

"Boots, huh? Okay, sounds interesting," I admit. But then, ever the skeptic, I say, "I do have two questions, though."

"Sure, what are they?"

"First, if the money is so great, why are you still working here at Applebee's? And second, why are you helping me?"

Blowing out a breath, Sammie says, "Honestly, I stay here for a few shifts each week because I feel bad for Barb. We really are incredibly short-staffed, and she is so nice and accommodating to whatever you need. I hate to leave her in a lurch, but I probably will quit at some point."

I nod. "All right, that makes sense. And reason number two?"

Sheepishly, she says, "Um, I actually get a referral bonus for anyone that I send in that gets hired at Boots."

I laugh. "Ah, got it."

Scrunching up her face, she asks, "Are you mad?"

"No, not at all." I shake my head. "I think it's smart of you to do a little recruiting for extra cash."

I like this girl.

We talk a little more, and I'm sold on trying for a job at this Boots establishment.

Since I'm not busy, and she's going there anyway, I decide to follow her down to the place.

Pulling into their lot, I determine that it looks respectable enough. Boots is just a basic restaurant with an Old English pub feel about it, nothing tawdry.

We park and go in, and I meet Sammie's manager, Annie.

It's funny. She takes one look at me and hires me on the spot.

When she walks away to retrieve the new hire paperwork I'll need to complete and bring back, Sammie and I look at each other and laugh.

"That was easy," I say.

"Told you you'd be a perfect fit, Ellie."

"Yeah, I guess you were right."

After Annie returns and gives me the paperwork, I say good-bye to Sammie and head out.

On my way home, I call Barb to give her the bad news. But she sounds so sad that I feel guilty and tell her I'll pick up a shift or two each week.

Hey, if Sammie can do it, so can I.

This is better anyway. I don't really want to share with Nils that I'm working at Boots. I bet he knows the place. In fact, I have a feeling every male within a fifty-mile radius knows about Boots.

And not that I think Nils would care, but he may tell Arden.

That would not be good, as my overprotective brother would certainly not approve. He'd worry too much about me.

So, for the foreseeable future, as far as Nils and Arden are concerned, I'm working solely at Applebee's.

Chapter

Ten

NILS

When I return from our road trip, I step into the entry hall of my house, drop my bags on the floor, and let out one long, relieved sigh.

Yeah, it's good to be home.

For a beat, I forget I no longer live alone. But I'm quickly reminded when I catch sight of a raven-haired whirlwind that's—*shit!*—about to slam right the fuck into me.

"Whoa, Ellie!" I grab her elbows as she skids to a stop in front of me. Steadying her, I chuckle and say, "Someone's in a hurry."

She takes two steps back, and my hands fall to my sides.

Breathing rapidly, she gasps, "Oh my God, I am so, so sorry. I almost took you out."

I chuckle. "No, I'm fine. But that was a pretty solid almost-check there, my friend."

Now she's laughing right along with me as she says, "Bet you weren't expecting that enthusiastic of a welcome back, huh?"

I know she's kidding, but a part of me wishes she really were that excited to see me return.

Dismissing that thought, because it's ridiculous, I tell her, "No, I can't say that I was."

"Well…" She smiles at me. "Welcome home, Nils."

"Thanks."

Since I finally have a chance to really take a good look at her, I do.

First, she's looking as hot as ever. Even though she has on simple black pants and a black polo shirt, her body is bangin'.

But I do have to wonder why she's dressed the way she is. Her outfit is definitely something a server at a restaurant might be wearing.

And then I see the logo.

Brow creasing, I cock my head and ask, "Did you get a job at Applebee's?"

She nods. "As a matter of fact, I did. And actually"—she holds her phone up to check the time—"I hate to run, but I'd better get going or I'm going to be so late. That's why I was in such a hurry and almost ran into you."

I have so many questions, like why did she get a job so quickly? But it's really not my place to ask. I guess I was just hoping to spend some time with her today. It's only noon, and it's really nice out. I was going to suggest that we hang out by the pool in the back of my house for a while.

Fuck, okay, I admit it—I'm dying to see her in a bikini. And yeah, I decided over the past few days that even though I can never have Ellie in any kind of sexual way, I can certainly still fantasize about her.

Not that I could stop myself from doing so anyway.

Yeah, that ship has sailed.

Trying to hide the disappointment in my voice, I say, "Oh, okay. You'd better go. I don't want to keep you."

Even though hanging by the pool is out, we still have this evening. Maybe she and I can spend some time together then.

In an even tone, seeing as I don't want to sound completely desperate, I ask, "What are you doing later tonight? We could watch another movie here at the house if you're not working too late."

Her turquoise eyes light up, and I swear my heart skips a beat. "Ooh," she says, "I'm definitely up for watching a movie. I'm done at six, so maybe we can plan for around seven?"

"Seven works for me," I say with a smile.

"Cool. See you then." She starts toward the door, but then she turns back. "Oh, and if you want to order pizza this time, I'd be cool with that. I didn't have time to eat anything for lunch, so I know I'll be starving after work."

"Sure," I reply. "I'll probably be grabbing a bite after you leave, but I'll be sure to skip dinner. By seven, I'll be nice and hungry too."

"Awesome, then pizza will be perfect."

"It will be," I agree.

She walks out the door, waving. "See you later, Nils."

I give her a little wave back. "Yeah, bye. See you tonight."

She leaves, and the house feels empty. I never cared or noticed how quiet it is around here in the past. But Ellie has such life to her. She has a way of filling the entire room with her presence and positive energy.

Letting out a sigh, I pick up my bags and take them upstairs. It's time to not only put my shit away, but also to table any further thoughts of Ellie.

As the day passes, I'm moderately successful in not thinking too much about the woman I'm sharing my house with. I must confess, though, that when I do spend some time out by the pool, I keep imagining her lounging next to me, clad in a skimpy bikini that matches her turquoise eyes.

I wonder if she has one in that color.

I should ask her when she gets home, which should be any minute now.

Yeah, like that would be a good idea, perv.

I focus instead on the time. It's after six, and as I promised Ellie, I'm hungry—like really fucking starving. I skipped dinner, and the thought of a nice cheesy pizza has my stomach growling.

We have practice tomorrow morning, so I'll easily burn off all the excess carbs and calories. Plus, I got in a light workout in my home gym about an hour ago.

I'm now showered and up in my bedroom, pulling a black tee over my head and zipping up my jeans.

As I pad out into the hall in my bare feet, I hear the beeping sound of the alarm being disarmed downstairs.

Yes! Ellie is home!

Quit getting so excited about her, dude. You're worse than some teenage kid with a crush.

I try to squash my enthusiasm, but as I start down the stairs, I accept that I obviously do indeed have a crush on Ellie. And it's a big one at that. Hopefully, it'll go away at some point and we can just be good friends.

That's a relationship Arden would approve of.

And I'll win my bet with Finn for sure, then.

I'm smiling at the thought of victory when I reach the base of the stairs.

Ellie, peering over at me with a smile of her own, quips in a teasing tone, "Well, it's not quite the 'welcome home' I gave you this morning, but a smile is always nice. Did you miss me?"

"Actually, I did," I just flat-out admit. "It was too damn quiet around here all day."

Clearly pleased with my admission, her smile widens. "Aww," she coos, "I think you just made my day, Nils."

As I rest my hand on the wooden newel post, I raise a brow and ask, "How was work? Was it rough…or not too bad?"

She shrugs. "It was all right. Not too hectic, but busy enough that I pulled in some decent tips. Still, I'm definitely looking forward to chilling tonight."

Hmm, if she wants to work, that's great. But I don't want her thinking she needs to pay me anything. Even though we discussed it before, I feel compelled to bring it up again.

"Hey, Ellie," I say.

"Yeah?"

"You remember how we talked about you not owing me any rent or anything like that for staying here, right?"

Shifting from one foot to the other, she says, "Yes, I remember."

"Well…" I blow out a breath. "I meant that. I truly don't want anything."

Except for maybe one night with you, my traitorous dick chimes in.

"Shut up," I grumble super softly so she can't hear.

But Ellie catches my murmuring and asks, "What was that?"

I try to refocus her on the first part of what I said. "Oh, I was just reiterating that you don't owe me anything."

I swear, the way she cocks her head and the knowing twinkle in her turquoise eyes tell me she's catching on to my raging internal battle.

Nodding, she says, "Yeah, I heard that part. And okay, but I still plan to buy some food and pay for a few pizzas along the way. In fact, I've already decided that I'm covering the tab tonight."

Thank God, it seems my redirection is working.

Keeping her on track, I make a big show of giving in, sighing and rolling my eyes. "All right, you can treat, if you really want to."

"I do," she says, "but before we get started…" She gestures down to her black server clothes. "Do you mind if I grab a shower and change first? I feel like I smell like a cornucopia of foods over here."

I can't smell anything from where I'm standing, but she's probably right.

Chuckling, I say, "Sure, of course." I point down the hall. "I'll wait for you in the entertainment room. Take your time, though."

"Okay."

I walk out into the hall, and she heads past me and up the stairs.

Once I'm settled on the sofa in the entertainment room, I turn on the TV and tune in to a sports channel so I can get caught up on any hockey news.

There's nothing groundbreaking, so I kind of zone out. I'm expecting to be waiting a while, as I know some women take forever to get ready. But it's not long at all before I hear Ellie padding down the hall.

I sit up straighter and turn toward the doorway so I can watch her as she walks in.

Holy shit, she's so damn pretty.

Does she always have to look so good?

Or maybe it's just me?

No, she looks fantastic. Her long dark hair is flowing over her shoulders, the soft curls at the ends bouncing lightly as she walks toward the sofa. And damn, the ripped jeans she has on are just snug enough to show off her long, lean legs and slim hips. Then there's her V-neck top. It's not the bikini I fantasized about earlier, but it is turquoise and brings out the color of her eyes as much as I imagined a swimsuit in that color would.

As she plops down on the sofa—close to me, but not as close as I'd like—my eyes are drawn to her cleavage. Only a hint of her perfect, rounded breasts is visible, but it's enough to make my dick twinge.

Okay, settle down, boss.

I quickly pick up my phone and say, "How about we order that pizza? I'm fucking starving."

For you, I think but wisely don't add.

"Sounds good to me." She slips her phone out from her jeans pocket. "Where are we ordering from? I'll pull up their menu too."

I tell her, and together we scroll through the options on our respective phones.

I like the way she kind of leans toward me on the sofa as we discuss whether to go for thin crust or thick—thick wins—and what kind of toppings we want.

"I'm good with just about anything," I share. "Just no pineapple."

Scrunching her pert little nose, she agrees, "Yeah, no pineapple for me either. Yuck."

We ultimately decide on a pizza with extra cheese, pepperoni, and mushrooms, along with two bottled sodas. I don't put up a fuss when Ellie insists that we place the order on her phone so she can use her Apple Pay.

"Okay, all right," I say. "But I've got us next time."

She agrees, and then we make a joint decision to wait to start a movie until the pizza arrives.

After the order is placed, we put away our phones, and she shares with me, "I'm so happy you like mushrooms. Arden hates them, so growing up, and even now if we order pizza, I can never, ever get them."

"You don't have to worry about that with me," I reply. "I love 'em." And then teasing, I look over at her and deadpan, "I guess you could say I'm a real 'fungi.'"

"Oh, God." She rolls her eyes, but she's chuckling too. "You did not just say that."

Shit, I'm turning into a true nerd around her.

But I don't even care, as my corny line made her laugh.

Shrugging, I admit, "Yeah, I totally did."

She shakes her head, then sits up straighter.

Running her hands down her jean-clad thighs, she says, "So, while we're waiting for the pizza, tell me more about you."

I nod. "Okay. What do you want to know?"

"Hmm…" She thinks it over, then says, "Let's start with the basics. Like, where did you grow up, and do you have any siblings?"

"Those are easy enough. I grew up in a little suburb just outside Minneapolis, Minnesota. And as for siblings, I don't have any."

"Lucky you," she snorts. "Bet you could always get mushrooms on your pizza if you wanted to."

I laugh. "Yeah, I guess I could have."

Sighing, she says, "Since Arden is your friend, I think you know my answers to those questions."

"Yeah, I do," I admit. "You grew up in Toronto, and Arden, the mushroom hater, is your only sibling."

"Yep, you got it."

I decide to get a little personal and ask, "What about boyfriends? There's no guy pining away for you back in Chicago, is there?"

I kind of know there's not, but I'm curious to learn if there's ever been anyone she's been in love with.

Scoffing, she says, "Nils, I wasn't even in Chicago long enough to meet the freaking mailman, let alone someone to date. But prior to that..." She blows out a breath. "As an undergrad, there were a couple of guys over the years who I was involved with. Nothing ever got super serious, though. I was always too busy with school and work. No one wants to be, like, your third priority, you know?"

"That's true," I agree. "I think that's why I haven't settled down. There have been a couple of serious girlfriends over the years for me, but those relationships always fizzled out. Hockey is my primary focus, and they just weren't okay with that."

She nods. "I totally understand. I know once I decide what I want to do school-wise and career-wise, I'll be putting everything I have back into those things." She sighs softly as she glances over at me. "Guess we definitely need partners who can understand that, huh?"

I catch her gaze and hold it. "Yeah, I think we do."

Silence descends, but it's a comfortable one as we share something with our eyes. Like, maybe we're a lot alike. And maybe we're the type of people we've both been looking for.

And maybe, just maybe—

Riiinnnggg!

Huffing, Ellie looks away. "That must be the pizza," she murmurs dejectedly.

"I'm sure it is." I stand as I let out a sigh. "I'll go get it."

The fucking doorbell has broken whatever spell we were falling under.

But maybe that's for the best.

No, it definitely is.

Chapter

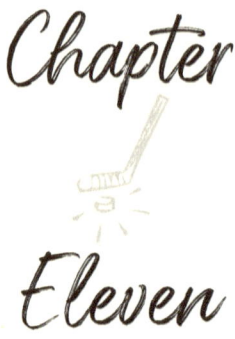

Eleven

ELLIE

Damn, what a loud-ass doorbell Nils has. And it just has to ring when we're clearly having a moment.

But now the connection has been ruined, so I huff and look away. "That must be the pizza," I mutter.

"I'm sure it is." He sighs as he stands up. "I'll go get it."

As I wait for Nils to return, I think about how we really do need partners in our lives who understand our passions. Like, I may be figuring things out, but what I told him is true. Once I have a new direction, which may even end up being my old direction, I plan to be 100 percent committed to it.

"That doesn't mean you can't have someone special in your life," I remind myself softly.

It's true, and saying it out loud makes it more of a possibility.

Wouldn't it be wild if Nils is that person for me?

And I'm the one for him?

I mean, hockey is his number one priority, and I'm fine with that. Or I could be.

"I could," I say out loud with a smile. "I definitely could."

"What could you do?" Nils asks as he returns to the room, pizza held high in one hand and two bottles of Coke intertwined in his fingers in the other.

Damn, that man has excellent hearing.

"Er, uh, um…," I stammer as I try to come up with some plausible explanation. And then I do. "I was just saying to myself that I bet I could eat more pizza than you."

"You think so, huh?" He raises a brow as he sets the pizza box and Cokes down on the coffee table. "Are you sure enough that you really would bet on it?"

Oh crap, I've trapped myself in a corner now. I'm hungry, yes, but as I eye the extra-large pizza box on the table in front of me, I'm not sure I can outeat this man.

Nils goes on. "You know, some hockey players love to bet on things."

I laugh. "And just why do I have a feeling you're one of them?"

"Because I am," he states proudly, puffing out his chest. "So, are you up for a little wager or not?"

I don't know what I'm getting into, but I go ahead and say, "Yes, I am."

I kind of have to at this point.

Nils, looking pleased that we're wagering, says, "Okay, first, before I put out there what I want if I win, I have to ask if you're working tomorrow."

"Nope." I shake my head. "I'm off. Well, wait, until the evening. I have a short shift then."

I don't elaborate that it's actually my training session at Boots that I need to go to. That must remain a secret.

Nils sounds über-excited as he exclaims, "Great! This will work, then. I only have a morning practice, and what I have in mind won't go into the evening."

"Okayyy," I draw out. "Go on."

Looking pumped, he states, "If I win, you have to promise to spend the day tomorrow out back at the pool with me. It's supposed to be beautiful, even warmer than today."

Hell, I'd spend the day with him anywhere, including at the damn pool even if it was raining. But I won't share that with him.

Putting on a neutral expression, I say nonchalantly, "I can agree to that."

I almost kind of want to lose now, but I still have a chance to get something I want if I win.

What should that be?

Tickets to an upcoming Thunder game?

No, I can get those anytime from Arden.

Access to their locker room?

Nah, same deal—Arden can make that happen too.

So, what do I want?

Hmmm, what I'd really like to ask for is for Nils to kiss me.

Just once.

And a really good one at that.

But I can't say that.

First, I want him to do it on his own, not because he has to.

Yeah, I need the idea to come from him.

Plus, it'd be better if it just sort of happened.

So, sighing, I stick with a boring, safe bet, one I have a feeling will extra-motivate him to win so we can hang at the pool tomorrow.

"If I win," I say, acting like the idea really excites me, "you have to go clothes shopping with me. Yay, right?"

"Yay?" He grimaces. "More like 'ugh.' Is that what you really want?"

I nod decisively. "It is, for sure."

He sighs as he flips open the pizza box. "Oh hell, I'd better win, then. Let's get this thing started."

"You got it."

As we begin our pizza eat-off, I'm feeling pretty damn smug. Despite my competitive nature urging me to gobble down as many slices as I can, I really don't care to win.

First, I hate clothes shopping! And second, I *want* to hang at the pool tomorrow with Nils.

So I throw the challenge.

I eat three slices, and he devours five.

"Looks like I won," Nils declares victoriously as he tosses a single piece of crust into the empty pizza box.

I don't push that he should technically be required to eat that too. It doesn't matter, though, as five beats three.

"Yes…" I take a swig of soda, swallow, and set the plastic bottle down on the coffee table. "You did. You won fair and square."

With victory in his hands, Nils is so pleased with himself that he tells me I can pick the movie.

"Anything at all?" I ask, raising a brow.

"Sure, it's your choice."

"Even a chick flick?"

He groans but concedes, "Even a chick flick."

I decide not to torture him, though. After zooming through a multitude of selections on the screen, I choose a comedy.

"Is this okay?" I ask.

Looking relieved, he states, "Perfect."

The movie is decent, and it has some good laughs, but the whole time we're watching it, I'm only half paying attention. I'm too busy thinking about our pool day and how much fun it'll be. I'm also trying to decide which of my many bikinis to wear tomorrow.

I think I need to wear one that's über-sexy, as I want to capture Nils's attention. In fact, I think I'll go with the skimpiest I own, a hot pink number that leaves little to the imagination.

That sly choice may just get me one step closer to winning what I really wanted to bet for tonight—a kiss from Nils.

Chapter

Twelve

NILS

Thank fuck I won that bet last night. Not only do I despise clothes shopping, but now Ellie will be joining me out here at the pool any minute.

It's really warm today. Muggy too. It's a good day to spend outside, except for one minor drawback. Despite the original forecast of clear skies, it looks like a thunderstorm is on the horizon. Dark clouds are rolling in, blocking out the sun at the moment, and they certainly look threatening.

I wish Ellie would hurry up and get out here. It's going to suck if the rain arrives before she does. Our day at the pool will be over before it even begins.

I don't want that.

Huffing, I sit up a little and shift in the pool lounger, adjusting my navy blue swim trunks before I lean back once again.

When I hear the sliding glass doors leading from the kitchen opening, I turn and…

Holy fuck!

Good thing I have on sunglasses. Otherwise, Ellie would surely see my eyes bulging out of my head. As it is, I have to quickly close my mouth.

"Hey," she says all calmly as she strides over wearing the hottest, sexiest, fucking skimpiest hot pink bikini I think I've ever seen.

"Hi." I give her a little wave as I swallow hard and try not to blatantly ogle her supple, beautiful breasts, flat stomach, and long legs.

As she sits down in the lounger next to me, I'm successful at keeping my eyes diverted. That is, until she asks me to pass the sunscreen.

Fuck.

"Yeah, sure," I mutter as I hand the bottle to her.

I'm thankful once again for the dark glasses I have on, as I'm able to surreptitiously watch her smooth the lotion up and down her legs, on her stomach, and—*kill me now*—all over her luscious chest and cleavage.

I'm tempted to ask if she needs me to help her rub it in.

Okay, that's my cock talking.

I have to turn away.

He likes looking at her a little too much, and if I continue, that fucker is going to get hard and give me away.

"Here you go. Thanks. I'm glad you had some down here." She hands me the sunscreen bottle and lowers the sunglasses I didn't even notice she had up on her head. "I forgot to put any on upstairs. And even though it's cloudy, those rays still get through."

"They do," I agree huskily as I place the sunscreen back on the ground.

I'm still a little worked up, so I just lean back and close my eyes, enjoying the warmth and just the right amount of breeze.

"It really is nice out today," Ellie says. "I think I like it better a little overcast. No glaring sun is great, you know?"

I open my eyes long enough to glance at her. Just her face, though. "It is nice," I agree, closing my eyes again. "Good thing I won that bet, huh?"

"Yeah, but..." She sighs as she slides the sunglasses back up on her head. "Can I be honest?"

Now I don't just open my eyes and peer over at her, but I lower my glasses as well.

"Of course," I say.

Meeting my gaze with those damn stunning turquoise blues, she says, "I would have hung out at the pool today with you anyway, Nils. All you had to do was ask."

Chuckling, I say, "Now you tell me. So, I could have chosen something else for our wager?"

"You could have, for sure," she confirms, lowering her sunglasses to the bridge of her nose. "And for the record, I have one more confession."

I'm dying to know what this one could be, so I ask, "What's that?"

She pauses, and then, trying to suppress a grin as she doesn't look over at me, she says, "I hate shopping."

"No way!" I blurt out. "You do?"

She nods once as she finally looks back over. "I do. I despise having to go to stores. I'd much rather shop online."

"Shit, man, me too." I throw my hands up in the air for dramatic emphasis. "That's why I fucking had to win. Though now you tell me I didn't really need to."

Soothingly, she says, "You did win, though. Fair and square."

Something doesn't add up, so I ask, "Why did you choose clothes shopping if you hate it so much?"

A definite blush creeps over her cheeks, and it's not from the sun, as she shrugs and says, "I don't know. I just couldn't think of anything else."

Hmm, I call bullshit. Her blushing tells me something different from what she's saying. But what could she have been thinking of as a bet that would make her this embarrassed?

Fuck, I wish I knew.

It had to be something good.

I could ask, but I won't.

She'll tell me if she wants to.

But she doesn't. Instead, she starts talking about hockey, which is always a go-to for me.

"When's your next game?" she asks.

"Tomorrow night," I say excitedly. "If you want to go, just let me know. I can make it happen."

I'm sure Arden could as well. But I'd rather be the one to get her a ticket.

"Aw, man." She blows out a breath. "I'd love to, but I have to work."

I'm disappointed but still throw out, "What about Tuesday night? We have another home game then."

After thinking it over, she says, "Yeah, I can make it to that one. I'm off Tuesday. I'm having lunch with Willow and Arden that day, but my evening is wide open."

"Perfect." I smile at her. "I'll line up a ticket for you. Do you want to sit up in a luxury box? Or down in the players' family section?"

I'm careful not to call it the wives and girlfriends section, like most of us do.

"Put me up close," she tells me. "I like being near the action."

Damn, this girl is awesome.

"Okay, I'll get you a real close seat," I promise. "How about one that's right up along the glass?"

"Oooh." She nods excitedly. "I'd love that."

"Consider it done." I nod once. "I'll text you the QR code and the details once I get everything in order."

"Great. Thanks, Nils."

I'm happy that I can do something for her, and I'm beyond pumped that she'll be coming to one of our games.

We talk a little more about hockey, then just switch over to some random chitchat. Like always, there's such an amazing level of comfort with us. We can talk about anything or nothing at all, and it's still interesting.

Crazy, huh?

I feel like I've known Ellie forever.

She's that easy to talk with.

In fact, we're so immersed in conversation that neither of us pays barely any heed to how the skies are darkening and looking ominous.

But we sure take notice when the first big, fat, ice-cold raindrops fall on us.

"Eeek!" Ellie cries out as she scrambles to sit up and then stand. "This rain is freezing."

I jump up as well, and luckily I've been lying on a big fluffy towel, so I grab that and rush over to Ellie to wrap it around her.

"Thanks," she says as the rain starts really fucking pouring.

With my arm wrapped over her shoulders to keep the towel in place, because now the wind is kicking up, too, we race over to the sliding glass doors and step into the kitchen.

Unfortunately, or maybe fortunately—for me, at least—we get the parquet floor all wet. And with both of us scrambling to try to close the sliding door at the same time, Ellie loses her footing and, as it slams shut, she falls into me.

Her towel starts to drop, and, with me steadying her, we try to grab it at the same time.

It's a battle we both lose as the stupid thing falls to the floor.

And that's how we somehow end up face-to-face, our bodies almost touching.

Whoa.

We're so close to each other that I can feel the heat coming off of her.

With the way she just licked her lips as she stares at my chest, I'm certain she feels me in the same way.

Her nipples are hard from the cold rain, or maybe a little from me. I'd like to think so. In any case, the thin pink material isn't doing much to conceal the contour and outline or deep rose color.

Fuck.

She's so close that if I move one inch closer, our chests will be pressed together.

I want to move.

Oh, how I want to.

But I don't.

Neither of us does anything. We just kind of enjoy the moment as we stand still, listening to our almost-shared breaths and trying like hell not to let our eyes meet.

Because if they do…

Outside, the rain is still falling. The sound is soothing, like white noise, until a rumble of thunder gets in on the soundtrack.

And then a bolt of lightning rips through the sky.

We both jump, which makes us laugh.

I've never been more thankful for a thunderstorm, seeing as I was about to do something really stupid—like fucking kiss the girl in front of me.

And maybe do more.

Ellie lets out a little shiver, and instinctively, without thinking, I lift my hands and gently rub her upper arms.

"Are you cold?" I ask, my voice rough and gravelly.

Touching her is electric, and I want to just do it forever.

It'd be so easy to reach around to her back and untie her bikini, letting it drop away and exposing those luscious breasts…for me to lick and suck on and—

"A little," she croaks out, breaking me from my lustful reverie and reminding me to stop caressing her arms.

"Okay." I drop my hands from her. "This towel on the floor is soaked." I toe it away. "Let me go grab some dry ones."

"All right, thanks."

I pad over to the laundry room, leaving wet footprints in my wake.

I don't care; I'll clean up later.

The best thing for me to do right now is get away from Ellie for a few minutes to straighten out my head. Before I do something stupid, and she, caught up in the moment, too, doesn't stop me.

Then we'll both be fucked…in more ways than one.

Chapter

Thirteen

ELLIE

Damn, I just fucked up.

As I stand in the kitchen, shivering in my soaked bikini as Nils walks away to grab dry towels, I realize I just missed my chance. If I'd only looked up at him when we were standing so close, he probably would have kissed me.

No, I *know* he would have.

And isn't that what I want?

Isn't that why I wore my skimpiest bikini?

So why didn't I just…look…up?

I let out a sigh. I guess I got caught up in the moment, as well. It was a good one, a nice one, one filled with heat and longing. I kept staring at Nils's chest, so smooth, so sculpted, so hard. I wanted it pressed against me, sans bikini.

That body of his…shit, it's beyond hot. I checked him out so many times when we were out by the pool.

But I was coy about it.

I don't think he even noticed.

Maybe because he was too busy ogling me. Yeah, I caught him again and again. My bikini did the trick—he was in total lust.

But I definitely still want more than my original plan of a one-night stand.

Rethinking things as I stand here now, maybe not looking up at Nils, not meeting his gaze, was the right move. Our chemistry is there, yes. It's hot and electric. But if we let it build, when we do come together, it'll be so much better.

We're already establishing a good base of friendship. We genuinely get along. But I want Nils to feel even more for me. I want him to fall for me, kind of like I feel the first stirrings of falling for him.

I need to give it more time, though.

Lord knows I have a lot of that.

As I wrap my arms around myself to keep warm, Nils returns with the fresh towels.

"Looks like I'm back just in time," he says as he hands me one.

I start to swipe the towel up and down my legs as I reply, "You definitely are. I'm feeling a chill. Thanks."

"No worries."

Nils and I dry off, but it's still kind of cold standing in the kitchen in a damp bikini.

Plus, that moment we shared is still on my mind.

I think it's on his too. He looks a little uncomfortable.

We should really get away from each other for a little while. Before, seeing how skimpily clad we are, we have another moment that ends with us ripping off what little bit we have on and going at it on the floor.

Mmm, that would be fun.

Okay, time to go.

Clearing my throat, I say, "I don't know about you, but I'm freaking freezing. I have to get on some dry clothes."

He agrees quickly, "Yeah, same here."

I start to walk away first, but when I don't feel him following me, I turn back around.

That's when I catch him staring at my ass.

Snickering, I ask, "Are you coming?"

Pretending like he wasn't just busted, he looks away and mumbles, "Uh, I'm actually going to take a shower down here. The clothes I want to put on are in the downstairs bathroom."

Yeah, sure they are.

I suspect his excuse is just a cover. I bet he's going to freaking jack off in the bathroom down here.

The thought of him stroking his cock under the pulsating water makes me think getting off in the shower might be a good idea.

So, blowing out a breath, I rush off to do exactly that.

Later that day, I have my training session at Boots. Sammie, the girl who told me about the position, is my trainer. Since I work with her at Applebee's, I'm comfortable and at ease. It also helps that she's super nice and really funny. I like her a lot.

After writing down all of my measurements, she puts together my outfit from the supply they have on hand.

We're in the back room, which doubles as an employee lounge. But since she and I are alone, I just change into the white button-down blouse, short red-and-black plaid skirt over black boy shorts, and high-heeled black leather boots right where I am.

Once I'm fully dressed, I spin around in front of a long, full-length mirror on the wall.

The outfit is sexy as hell but still classy.

"You look fantastic," Sammie says.

"Thanks," I say, turning to face her.

Looking concerned, her forehead creasing, she asks, "Now are you sure feel comfortable dressed like that?"

"Pfft." I let out a laugh, thinking of the skimpy bikini I was wearing earlier today. Of course, that was mainly for Nils's sake. But still, I'm fine. I tell her as much and add, "I actually think this ensemble is really cute."

"It is," she agrees. "Just wait. I predict you're going to make a ton of tips out there."

She's right. I do really well for my first night. Sammie only had to train me on the basics, then I was pretty much on my own.

When I return home, I'm whooped, so I go upstairs and straight to bed.

I sleep in late the next day, so I don't run into Nils. Not for any bad reason. I remember him mentioning there was a team meeting at noon, and afterward he and some of his teammates were going to grab a bite to eat.

He has a game this evening, as well, the one I can't go to because of work.

Since my shift is at Boots, when it's time to get ready, I check the house to make sure Nils is still not home.

He's not, so I decide to just wear my "sexy" outfit to work. It's easier than changing there.

But when Nils is around, I'll be sure to wear the Applebee's uniform and take this one to Boots in a bag.

That way this job will remain a secret.

My evening shift goes by quickly. Boots is busy, and it feels like I'm moving nonstop.

At one point, when I make my way over to the bar to pick up a drink order, I run into Sammie. "Damn," I say, catching my breath, "it's crazy busy tonight."

"It is," she agrees as she loads her own tray with beverages. "The weekends are always like this."

"That's a good thing," I say.

She nods and rushes off.

It is a good thing, a very good thing, as my hectic night pays off. Not only does the time fly by, and the next thing I know, my shift is over, but I pull in a boatload of tips.

Once I go out to my car, before heading home, I check my phone to find out the score of the Thunder game.

"Yay, we won," I murmur happily when I see the result.

It's pretty late, and the game ended a while ago, so I assume Nils will be home and in bed. That means there's no need for me to sneak in and run upstairs to remain undetected in my Boots attire.

The drive home is quick and relaxing. I feel good. Things are going so well, with my new jobs and with Nils.

I park in the driveway, where I take notice that there are no other cars. I just assume Nils must've pulled into the garage.

"He better be asleep," I murmur as I hop out of my Jag and head up to the house.

I want to be careful, so I only step partway into the entry hall.

Everything is quiet and Nils is not around.

See, I was right.

I blow out a relieved breath.

I'm pretty sure I'm safe from running into him, as the only illumination is from a lamp on a stand against the wall, which is usually how he leaves this area once he goes to bed.

Feeling confident, I step all the way into the entry hall and gently place my car key fob into a bowl next to the lamp.

I let out another breath.

I can finally completely relax.

But then, before I can run off or move in any way, Nils freaking pads down the stairs, clad in a pair of dark lounge pants and nothing else.

With nowhere to hide, I freeze.

Why is he coming downstairs?

He looks like he was sleeping, or getting ready to.

Where can I go?

What can I do?

I look left and right.

I'm trapped!

As panicked as I am, I don't miss that Nils doesn't have on a shirt. I take a quick few seconds to admire his sculpted chest…corded arms…taut stomach—

"Ellie?"

Oh crap, he's at the bottom of the stairs now, and I'm like a deer caught in the headlights of an oncoming car.

"Er, uh…"

I look left and right again.

I have nowhere to go, no place to hide.

I am well and truly busted.

"Um," he goes on, cocking his head curiously, "not that it's any of my business, but why are you wearing a Boots outfit?"

Shit, he knows the place.

I make a face, then state, more as a question than a reply, "Because I work there?"

"You do?" He looks really confused now. "I thought you worked at Applebee's?"

I nod. "Yeah, I work there too. I, uh, actually work at both places."

He crosses his arms, making his muscles just freaking pop, so it takes me a beat to realize he just asked another question.

Making sure I'm not openly drooling, though internally I totally am, I say, "What was that?"

Smirking, he pauses.

Okay, I think he just figured out that I was ogling him.

He must, as he looks smug when he asks, "I said, why didn't you tell me you work at Boots too?"

"Oh."

I blow out a breath and decide to just be truthful.

What's the point in lying?

"It's just that, I don't want Arden to know," I explain. "He's such an overprotective brother sometimes. I'm worried he'll flip if he knows I work there."

Nils looks like he completely agrees as he sighs. "Yeah, he probably would be mad. But you do know hockey players go to that place, right? I'm talking guys from our team. There's a good chance you're going to be found out."

"I thought of that," I admit. "But a lot of them don't know me or that I'm Arden's sister."

He raises a brow. "And if one day Arden himself walks in?"

I shrug. "Then I guess I'm fucked. But until that day comes, and it may never"—I plead with my eyes—"will you please, please not say anything to him?"

Softly, he replies, "Of course I won't. I promise your secret is safe with me."

I release a relieved breath. "Thank you, Nils."

"You're welcome, Ellie."

I'm actually glad I came clean with him. It'll be easier not to have to sneak around. And now that I know I can trust Nils, I'm not concerned with Arden finding out. Despite what he said, I don't think my brother will ever step into Boots. It's just not his usual kind of go-to place.

With everything settled, I'm so relieved that I'm just ready to go to bed.

I tell Nils that I'm heading upstairs, but as I start toward the staircase, I'm curious about something.

Slowing to a stop, I cock my head and ask, "Why were you coming downstairs anyway? You look like you're ready for bed."

"I am," he says, "and I'm beat. But I forgot my phone in the kitchen."

"Ahhh," I breathe, "got it."

"And now that you reminded me," he goes on. "I'd better go get it."

Touching his arm lightly as he passes me, I say softly, "Good night, Nils."

Letting out a little sigh filled with regret or longing—I'm not sure which, but maybe both—he murmurs, "'Night, Ellie."

Chapter

Fourteen

NILS

The night I caught Ellie coming into the house in her Boots attire, we forged a secret…and a bond.

I've kept my promise to not tell a soul that she works at Boots. I have no intention of divulging that bit of info to anyone, certainly not her brother. Though I do worry she'll be found out at some point.

Still, it won't be because of me.

I'm proving to her that she can trust me.

Even though I remained nonchalant that night in the entry hall, inside, a spike of jealousy reared its ugly head. I can't help but hate that other guys get to see her dressed so fucking sexy.

The bikini she wore out at the pool covered less, but I was the only one who got to enjoy that.

So yeah, clearly sometimes I'm a possessive asshole.

And the girl isn't even mine.

I remind myself of that all the time, which is getting harder and harder to do. It seems that, as time wears on, I *want* her to be mine.

It started with our secret and the bond it created. Oh hell, that's not true. It started before that. But my desire for her has grown stronger.

And it's no longer about pure lust.

When Ellie came to the first game I got her a ticket for, she sat in the front row along the glass. I scored a beautiful goal right in front of her, and the way she jumped up and cheered, I felt like we'd just won the fucking Stanley Cup.

It made my heart soar that much.

Our eyes met as I headed to the bench to fist-bump my teammates.

I'll never forget that moment with her. It was brief but held so much emotion.

After that game, Ellie came down to the locker room. Not when we were undressing. She stopped in while the press reporters were still there. She claimed she was dropping in to say hi to Arden, but the funny thing was, she spent most of her time talking with me and Finn.

I was glad he was there. It was our chance to finally see if she flirted with him like she does with me.

She didn't.

She just talked with Finn the way you'd speak with someone you'd just met.

And when no one was looking, she bumped my hip with hers, winked at me, and said, "Great goal, by the way."

I replied with a soft and heartfelt "Thanks, Ellie."

She left shortly after that.

And guess what? Someone had caught our interaction after all.

Damn Finn.

Smirking, he leaned in and said to me in a low, mock-falsetto tone, "Great goal, by the way, you big, dreamy man."

"Oh, shut the fuck up," I hissed. "She did not say all that."

"She may as well have." He snorted. "I saw the way she was looking at you. And, dude…"

He trailed off, and that was the end of that conversation.

But I knew he was right.

It made me feel good, though.

But what was even more reassuring was that she hadn't flirted with Finn.

So it's not just the way she is.

It's the way she is with *me*.

You got that right!

Ellie has come to a few more games since then. I always try to get her a seat along the glass. She likes it, and that way we can make eye contact and sneak in a few sly smiles.

Also, she's up close and personal when I score a goal or get an assist. She still goes wild, too, cheering for me like I just conquered the world.

I love that.

Talk about motivating.

I guess that's why selfish me likes it best when she comes to the games by herself. A couple of times she's brought her friend Sammie. We had to play it cool then.

Oh, and one time, she came to a game with Willow. That really sucked, because they sat up in a luxury box. I couldn't see Ellie at all.

But I knew she was there.

And really, that's all that mattered.

More time passes, and October turns to November.

It feels like we finally have our early crazy lust-filled attraction under control.

Or maybe we just hide it better.

I know I do.

For as much as I've been on the road for away games with the team, Ellie and I still spend a good deal of time together.

I can say that we've truly become friends.

But in some ways, that's worse. My longing for her continues to grow into something more, something deeper. It's not just my body that wants her, anymore. My mind does too.

And dare I say my heart?

Fuck, I'm falling for her, aren't I?

Or maybe I've already fell.

All I know is that I don't even care anymore about that stupid bet.

I don't think Finn does either. He never mentions it. He hasn't since Ellie came to the locker room and he saw us interacting.

He knows this isn't a game anymore.

This shit is for real.

Today I finally have a chance to find out how he feels. We have a home game tonight, but right now, I'm meeting Finn for lunch.

In fact, he just pulled into the parking lot of the Italian restaurant we chose so we can carb-load for the game.

I'm already parked, so I get out of my SUV and walk over to meet Finn at his Escalade.

We go in together, and I notice he doesn't say one word about how he should be driving my Range Rover any day now.

I don't mention it, either.

But, after we're seated in a booth, I decide to bring up Ellie. We haven't had the chance to talk much about her, as it seems our teammates are always around, including Arden.

This is the first time in a while that it's been just the two of us.

We place our orders, and then I lean back and just bluntly state, "Hey, for the record, you haven't asked in a while, but I still haven't slept with Ellie."

Finn is taking a drink of water and almost chokes.

Clearing his throat and setting his glass down on the table, he says, "Wow, that just came out of nowhere. To be honest, I haven't even thought about that bet lately." He raises a brow. "Is it still on?"

I rub my forehead as I murmur softly, "I don't know."

"Why?" he asks, smirking. "Did something go down with you guys and I've actually already won?"

I'm not sure if he's serious or being a smartass, so I snap, "No, nothing has happened. Don't get all excited. The Rover is still mine."

Finn waves his hand. "Ah, dude, I'm just giving you a hard time. Really, though, fuck that bet. It was dumb to begin with."

"Are you serious?" I ask.

"For sure, I am. I can see something is going on with you and Ellie, something more than the standard 'we just want to fuck each other's brains out.'"

"Well, there is still that," I admit quietly.

"Yeah, but there's more," he states correctly. "And our friendship is far important than a fucking bet. So, talk to me, man."

When you take away all of the joking and jabbing at each other, Finn really is my friend.

He's a good guy.

I certainly can't talk to Arden about this, but I can with him.

So I will.

Peering over at Finn from across the table, I say, "I think I'm fucked, man."

He knows right away. "Shit, you've fallen for her, haven't you?"

I nod. "I have."

"So, how does she feel about you?"

I shrug. "I can't be certain, 'cause it's not like we've discussed it, but I think she feels the same way. I get that vibe from her, you know? We definitely have something building."

"I feel you." His brow creasing, he asks, "What's holding you back from taking things to the next level? Is it Arden?"

I let out a sigh and, leaning back even farther, I cross my arms. "Yeah, there's that, of course. I mean, I still don't want to be the guy who said he could be trusted who beds the man's sister. But also, like I said, I'm not 100 percent sure on how she feels. I don't even know what her plans for the future are. Hell"—I throw my hands up in the air—"for all I know, she could be going back to Chicago in January."

"Dude…" Finn blows out a breath. "Hasn't she said anything to you about what she's planning to do?"

I shake my head. "Not one word."

"Have you asked her straight up what her plans are?"

Sheepishly, I admit, "Um, not really."

"Okay." He blows out a breath. "So that's a hard no."

"It is," I confess. "But in my defense, the subject never comes up."

"Well, it needs to," Finn says. "You have to talk to her. At least about what she plans to do next. I mean, it's not like she's going to stay at your house forever."

I feel a pang in my heart, and I murmur softly, "What if I want her to? Would that be so awful?"

Our food arrives then, so the conversation ends.

But not before I hear Finn mutter under his breath, "Fuck, you've got it bad."

He's right about that, and he's also correct that I need to talk to Ellie.

Before I continue to allow myself to fall for her—not that I could stop even if I wanted to—I have to know she's not leaving.

At the very least, if she is, I need to back *way* the fuck off.

Spending any time with her at all will have to stop.

Chapter

Fifteen

ELLIE

I've been thinking a lot lately about what I want to do with my life. I've not said anything to anyone, as this is something I need to figure out by myself. Hell, it's why I came to Atlanta in the first place.

The good news is I think I've finally made a decision.

No, I have.

And I feel good about it—heart, soul, and mind.

Ever since I first arrived in town, I put everything on the back burner. That was fine…for a while. I was busy having fun flirting with and pursuing Nils.

But then shit got real with him. It was no longer fun and games. I've not only fallen for the man, I'm head over heels in love with him.

Only problem is, he doesn't know.

I think he's got it bad for me, too, but I'm not sure he feels as strongly as I do. I wish I could just ask him, but the truth is, I'm scared.

I'm even fearful to tell him I've made a decision on my future, which is that I'm staying in Atlanta.

I don't want him to think it has anything to do with him, though it partly does. But I'd stay even if nothing had ever developed between us. I just want to be close to Arden and Willow. They're family, and it soothes me to have them nearby.

But the most important reason I've made the decision to stay is because *I* like it here.

Atlanta feels like home.

I'm going to still pursue a career in law too.

I'll obviously need to apply to law schools down here, so I'll be taking one more semester off to get things in order.

Hopefully, I can start back next fall.

In the meantime, I'm keeping my jobs, including the one at Boots.

Thank goodness Nils has kept his word and hasn't told a soul about me working there. I've also lucked out that no hockey players have come in while I've been working.

So Arden still doesn't know.

I plan to keep it that way.

There is one other thing weighing on me, though. One uncertainty. I'm going to need to find a new place to live. I can't stay with Nils at his house forever.

But what if I want to?

I actually do.

We get along so well, and I'm comfortable here.

There's also that little thing that I've fallen for him.

There's nothing I can do to change that, nor do I want to.

That's why I need to talk to Nils soon. I'm not ready to lay my feelings on the line, but I should clue him in as to what my plans for the future are.

Maybe I'll bring it up tonight after his game, or possibly before. Sammie has to work, and Willow is staying home, so I'm going alone.

Well, not really alone. I'll be hitching a ride down to the arena with Nils. This way we can ride back to the house together after the game.

We've done it this way a few times before, and it works out nicely. First, why take two cars? And more importantly, Nils tells me driving home with me helps him decompress after the game. I enjoy hearing his inside perspective on how certain plays unfolded or went down, so that's a plus.

As much as I know about hockey, I've learned even more from Nils.

But tonight, instead of hockey talk, I'll let him know that I've decided on a direction for my future.

He's probably been wondering, so I'm curious as to how he'll respond.

I hope he's happy, because I sure am.

My good mood continues as I spend the remainder of the afternoon getting ready for the game. I eat a light late lunch down in the kitchen, then head upstairs to change into jeans, sneakers, and a black-and-silver Thunder hoodie over a black V-neck tee.

When I'm heading back downstairs, Nils is walking in the front door.

"Hey," I say, stopping on the bottom step. "How was lunch with Finn?"

"It was good," he replies as he sets his key fob in the bowl on the stand in the entry hall. Chuckling as he looks me over, he says, "Someone is ready for the game."

"You know it," I retort.

I think about bringing up my decision now, but Nils looks tired.

Sure enough, he yawns and says, "I think I'm going to get in my pregame nap now. We're still on for driving down to the arena together, right?"

"Yes." I nod. "Definitely."

"Cool."

Nils heads toward the stairs to go up and take his nap, and I make my way to the kitchen to clean up from lunch.

Yeah, I never did clear the table.

I get my cleaning in and spend some time catching up on my phone. The next thing I know, Nils is padding into the kitchen, asking me if I'm ready to go.

"Yep." I stand and stow my phone away in my jeans pocket. "Let's go."

On the way down to the game, we don't have a lot to talk about, just some random chitchat. So I determine this is a good time to bring up my plans.

Looking over at Nils as his eyes remain on the road, I clear my throat and say, "Hey, I wanted to tell you something. You're actually going to be the first to know."

"Wow, okay. I'm honored." Glancing over at me, he raises a brow. "What do you want to tell me?"

I blow out a breath, and then I announce, "I finally made a decision about my future."

He coughs, like he's surprised. "Whoa, no way, you did? Really? So, what did you decide?"

We're at a red light, and this time when he looks at me, there's a clear mix of excitement and trepidation in his expression. One thing for sure, he's invested in what I'm about to say.

That makes me feel better about my decision.

Smiling at him, I say softly, "I'm staying in Atlanta."

Nils breaks out into the biggest grin, one that is so genuine that it warms my heart.

"You are?" he asks quietly, like he needs to hear it again.

I nod and confirm, "Yes, I'm staying."

"What about law school?"

"I'm still going to go, but I'll need to apply to schools down here."

The light turns green, and, still smiling big and wide, he hits the gas.

As he drives, I fill him in on more of the details. But I hold off on mentioning anything about moving out.

He doesn't bring it up either.

I guess that'll be a conversation for another day.

That's fine. I'm enjoying how pleased he appears to be about my news.

As we near the arena, he slows and says, "This is really great, Ellie. I'm happy you're staying. Like, I'm truly fucking over the moon."

Wow.

My heart skips a beat.

Feeling more confident than I did before that I've absolutely made the right decision, I say, "You know what? I'm fucking over the moon that I'm staying too."

And it's no lie.

I am.

Chapter

Sixteen

NILS

Yes, yes, yes! *Ellie isn't leaving town!*

And I'm the first to know.

That makes me happy in a way I can't even put into words.

Good thing she told me while I was driving. If I hadn't been behind the wheel, and she over in the passenger seat, I may not have been able to stop myself from grabbing her up in a massive hug, lifting her off her feet, and spinning her around.

That's how joyful I felt.

I'm still riding high, and we're near the end of the third period in our game against the Columbus Blue Jackets.

It's been a good matchup. There's not been a lot of defense but plenty of offense—we're up 6–4—which is always fun for the fans.

Time is winding down, and the Blue Jackets just pulled their goaltender.

It's getting a little chippy out on the ice, seeing as their players are feeling frustrated.

They've had some good opportunities, but our goalie has been solid. I'm confident that nothing is getting past him with just two minutes left in the game.

I'm on the blue line, and Arden just passed me the puck.

I make sure I'm the first going into the opponent's zone so we're not offside.

I accomplish that, and my linemates quickly follow.

Still, I'm ahead of everyone.

And I have a nice empty net staring at me.

I take my shot and the puck goes in, but in the same second, I feel a stick whack at my ankle, right where there's not a lot of padding.

"Fuck!" I scream as a stinging pain radiates from where some fuckhead Columbus player just slashed me.

I turn around and see him laughing.

My teammates race in, as do their guys, and the refs and linesmen have to separate everyone.

I'd like to fight the fucker myself, but a ref, the one who just called the penalty against him, is leading the jackass to the box.

My ankle is definitely fucked up, but I'm able to hobble-skate my way over to the bench.

Our trainer immediately takes me to the back room, where I'm evaluated by our medical team using a series of imaging and tests.

"So," I ask our team doctor from where I'm lying on the exam table in a tech tee and long black shorts, "how bad is it?"

Sternly, he says, "The good news is, your ankle isn't broken."

I blow out a sigh of relief and start to sit up.

"Whoa, hold on there." He places a hand on my shoulder, urging me to lie back down. "It's not all good news, my friend."

Ugh!

I run my hand down my face and ask, "Am I going to be out of the lineup?"

"Yes." He nods. "You may not have a break, but there is a small hairline fracture. We'll tape you up before you leave, and I'm going to give you a set of crutches. They're not for long term, but I'd like for you to not put too much weight on that ankle for a few days. It's going to heal on its own, but no skating for at least three weeks."

"Three weeks!" I cry out, and this time he's not quick enough to stop me from sitting up. "It's almost December. That means I won't be back playing until around Christmas. Is that right?"

"It's an accurate estimate," the doctor confirms.

"Great," I mumble. "Just great."

The only bright spot in this whole clusterfuck of a situation is that I'll get to spend some quality time with Ellie.

Funny how there was once a time that I avoided her. I can't even imagine that now. She's such a part of my life, and an important one at that.

That's why I was so happy earlier when she gave me the good news that she's staying in Atlanta. Even with the bad news of this injury, the thought of her not leaving me makes me smile.

Shit, wait till she hears I'm out of the lineup till late December.

I know she saw that opposing player slash my ankle, though I wasn't able to catch her reaction, since she was seated over on the other side of the arena.

I bet she's worried.

We planned to meet in the players' family lounge after I was showered and dressed, which is something I now still have to do.

I ask the doctor about that, and he recommends waiting to shower until I get home.

"Do you have someone there who can help you with things so

you can stay off your feet for a few days?" he asks.

"Help me with what? Showering?" I blurt out, my mind filling with images of me surely fucking my ankle up even more if Ellie were in the shower with me.

Yeah, I'd have her up against the tile, holding onto the wall—

"No," the doctor replies with a chuckle as he breaks me out of my lusty reverie. "I meant someone who can help you around the house with various things here and there."

"Yes." I nod, knowing Ellie will be more than willing to do whatever it takes to get me back on my skates and playing again.

She knows how important hockey is to me.

Before I leave, I get taped up.

And then I hobble down the hallway on my crutches to go find Ellie.

Chapter

Seventeen

ELLIE

I take time off from work for the rest of the week so I can help Nils around the house. He's on doctor's orders to stay off his feet for at least a few days.

God, he looked so sad when he made his way into the family lounge at the arena last night. I was damn worried after I saw that hit to his ankle. I feared the worst. Though a hairline fracture is nothing to take lightly, at least it's not a break.

Still, he'll miss some games.

Nils was in surprisingly good spirits on the way home, but only after I told him I was going to take some time off to help him. I caught him over in the passenger seat smiling when he heard that.

He was funny then too.

As I drove us home, he kept apologizing for smelling bad, telling me, "I'm sorry I didn't have a chance to shower at the arena." Waving his hand around, he joked, "We're probably going to have to air this thing out tomorrow morning."

"For sure," I teased, holding my nose. "I think so."

"Heyyyy," he retorted. And then, looking worried, he asked, "Is it really that bad?"

"No." I shook my head. "Not at all. I was only joking."

He seemed relieved, like he wouldn't want to repulse me. But he was fine; he only smelled a little extra manly. To be honest, it kind of turned me on. So much so that once we were back at the house and he told me he was going to head upstairs to take a shower, I had half a mind to follow him, sneak in his bathroom, and "help."

Yeah, I could have assisted him in soaping up his chest, trailed my hands down his sculpted abs, and then moved a little lower, lower—

"Ellie? Ellie, did you hear me?"

Oops, I forgot I'm currently sitting at the kitchen table with Nils, having breakfast.

"Wait, what?" I stare over at him blankly.

"Didn't you just hear that?' he asks, looking at me curiously. "The toast popped up."

"Oh? Ohhh…" My face is hot, and I know I'm blushing, so I jump up as fast as I can to grab the toast to go along with the scrambled eggs and bacon I made for us.

I walk back over to the table and plop a toasted piece of bread on the side of his plate.

Then I sit back down.

Cocking his head and peering over at me intently, Nils asks quietly, "What were you thinking about?"

Shit, he looks like he really wants to know, and that he suspects it was something sexual. The tension between us lately has been ratcheting up, and the only things keeping it at bay are his hockey games and my work.

But now it's just going to be the two of us, alone and together for twenty-four seven.

Help!

I'm going to need to stay strong and not just attack him. That's why there's no way I'm telling him I was imagining soaping him up in the shower.

He may suggest we try it.

And I may agree.

No, I know I would.

Waving my hand, I say nonchalantly, "Oh, it was nothing."

He raises a brow. "Really? 'Cause whatever it was, you're still blushing about it."

Damn red cheeks!

"I am?" I croak out.

"Yeah, you are." He takes a bite of toast and shrugs.

Swishing my hand in front of me, I say, "I guess my face is red because it's kind of hot in here."

Pausing, toast poised in his hand, he looks over at me.

Wow, though it wasn't all that warm before, when our eyes lock, it does indeed go up a few degrees.

I guess he feels the heat, too, since Nils says, "You got that right."

Before I say something I'll regret, like "Freaking kiss me now or I may die," I drop my gaze to my plate and pretend like it takes all my concentration to scoop up some scrambled eggs with my fork.

We eat in silence, which is exactly what we need, so the fire between us can cool to its usual mild simmer.

Now if we can just keep it this way for the next few days that I'm off.

Then we'll be in the clear.

The rest of the week passes, and we do a pretty good job of keeping our usual flirtation under control.

Nils's ankle is doing much better—no more crutches or limping around—but the doctor does tell him not to skate yet, which leaves him feeling bummed.

I feel bad for him, so I take a couple of extra days off. I'm having so much fun having Nils all to myself that it's an easy decision.

Since the Thunder are out of town on a short two-game road trip, Nils and I watch both games on the big-screen TV in the entertainment room.

Man, I can tell he can't wait to get back on the ice.

During the game we watched last night, the guy from the minors who got called up to replace him on his line was beaten really badly on a play, and the other team scored.

"I could have prevented that," he muttered dejectedly.

"I bet you would have," I replied, hoping to cheer him up. "Look at it this way: at least your job's not in jeopardy."

That got a laugh, but also a resigned sigh.

I wanted so much to scoot over and place my arm around him to comfort him, but I didn't dare do that. We're being extra careful now since we're together all the time. One wrong move—or would it be a *right* one?—and we could very well end up ripping each other's clothes off and going at it on the floor.

Yeah, there is that much sexual tension.

There was a time when I would have been fine with a quick romp, but I still want more. If something were to ever happen between us, I need to know it'll mean as much to Nils as it will to me.

If it doesn't, our whole friendship could be ruined.

I don't want that.

Despite our best efforts, though, we're reaching a point where something has to give. One of us needs to take a chance and make a move.

It may be me, and tonight could be my perfect opportunity.

Nils and I are going to a holiday laser show that's out in a big farm field in the country. Though we'll be parked in my car, as I'm going to drive my Jag, we've already decided we'll have a better view if we get out of the car and lean against the bumper.

So, even though I'm planning on wearing hiking boots, jeans, a thick sweater over a turtleneck, and a jacket, I may still get cold.

And that right there could be my opportunity.

I just hope that if it presents itself, I'm brave enough to take it… and that it goes well.

Several hours later, Nils and I are parked in the farm field, watching different colored lasers blast across the sky in time to holiday music.

It's actually pretty cool.

And kind of chilly, like, for real.

I don't have to pretend I'm cold like I thought I might.

Brrr…

Nils and I are in front of my car, leaning back against it. We have the windows down so we can hear the stereo blaring out the music synchronized to the laser show.

There are several other cars in the field, but we are all evenly spaced. There's actually plenty of room in between vehicles, so it doesn't feel crowded at all.

The wind picks up a bit, and I start to shiver.

I move closer to Nils, narrowing the gap between us to mere inches.

I'm not making a move; I really do need his body heat.

Okay, and I do like being close to him like this.

Glancing over, he asks, "Are you cold?"

I shudder and murmur, "A little."

"Do you want to get in the car?"

I think about it, but the view is so much better out here, so I say, "Not really."

Nils sighs. "We probably should have brought a blanket with us. Do you have one in the trunk?"

I shake my head. "No, but I should."

"No worries." He slips off the khaki field jacket he's wearing. "I have an idea." Wrapping it around my shoulders, which helps a lot, he asks, "Is that better?"

"Much. What about you, though?" I jerk my chin to indicate how he only has a checkered flannel over a black T-shirt to keep his upper body warm.

Nonetheless, he insists, "I'm fine."

Minutes later, though, he's crossing his arms and blowing out a breath that is clearly visible.

His jacket is big over my shoulders anyway, so I hold out one arm of it and raise a brow. "Do you want to share?"

As he bites his lip, I see a battle raging behind his eyes.

But then he mutters, "Fuck it," and slips under the jacket with me.

Only problem is, though his coat is large, it's not big enough to cover across the back of both of our shoulders.

And it keeps slipping down.

I'm worried he'll just give the jacket back to me and deal with the cold, but then he says, "Hey, if you're okay with it, I have another idea."

"Sure, what is it?"

Taking control of the situation with no more hesitancy, which I love, Nils positions me in front of him, wraps his coat around his back, then murmurs in my ear, "Lean back, Ellie."

Oh my God, I do, and the warmth of his solid body alone is way better than the jacket by itself. I'm not anywhere near cold, especially when he wraps his strong arms around me, encircling my body.

Sighing, I relax back into him even farther.

I feel him breathing into my hair as he rests his chin on my shoulder.

And then he turns his head slightly, and his warm breaths are tickling my neck.

I sigh, and he asks, "Is this okay?"

"Uh-huh," I breathe out.

He trails his nose up along the side of my neck to my ear, where he whispers, "What about this?"

Time stops.

I feel only him.

This is heaven.

The rainbow of lasers and pulsating music only add to the intensity of the moment.

I nod and croak out, "Yes."

Slowly, he turns me around to face him.

Damn, I am putty in his hands. And I want him to mold me and shape me.

Blinking once, I look up into his eyes, the lasers reflecting back in his green depths.

But there's more, so much more in his gaze—capitulation, surrender, and a sense that there's no going back.

Good. I don't want to go back.

I want to move forward.

I'm confident too. I know now, with my eyes locked with his, that if we take things to the next level, it'll mean as much to him as it will for me.

Swallowing hard, he says, "I've wanted to kiss you for so fucking long. But I've never wanted to as much as I do right now."

"So do it," I breathe out.

With a growl, his lips touch mine. It's a soft graze at first, a gentle brushing back and forth, like he's testing me. Then he sucks in my lower lip, pulls, pushes back in…

I go with it, letting him set the pace, until our mouths are open and our tongues are touching.

Sighing, I snake my arms around his neck.

He pulls me closer, and I feel every muscle, every hard ridge, and every defined line.

Gah!

We break apart, gasping and breathing hard, and I tell him, "I want you."

"Fuck, girl, I've wanted you since day one."

"Then let's get out of here."

"Hell, yeah!"

Chapter

Eighteen

NILS

This is everything I've been fighting against, everything I said would never happen. I vowed to not make any moves on Arden's sister. I certainly never planned on kissing her.

It didn't matter how much I wanted Ellie. I was committed to staying strong.

And yet here we are.

You know what, though?

I don't care.

I'm done fighting.

I'm done keeping my feelings a secret.

I fucking love Ellie Troy.

That's right; I said "love."

And tonight I'm going to show her just how much.

I drive us home, even though we're in her car. I don't think she could drive if she wanted to. She's all over me, running her hands up and down my jean-clad thighs. And now she's kissing my neck and the side of my stubbled face.

Though I love it, I have to say, "Babe, if you keep that up, we're going to wreck."

"Then get us home faster," she grinds out as she squeezes my leg.

Oh hell, I hit the gas.

Boy, do I ever.

We make it to the house, but pulling into the garage and parking is a blur.

Walking into the house is too.

At some point—fuck the ankle, especially since it feels a lot better anyway—I pick Ellie up in my arms and carry her to my bedroom.

I kick the door closed behind me, and then our clothes are discarded all over the damn place.

At one point, I grab the comforter on the bed and just rip it the hell off.

There are giggles and laughs, like when I almost trip over that damn comforter, or when I have Ellie prone on the bed and I'm kneeling above her, yanking off one of her cute, fuzzy pink socks, and it goes flying across the room.

I almost lose my balance, but I recover quickly.

When we stop and look into each other's eyes, we know that what's finally happening is so fucking right.

"I've been waiting so long for this," I confess. "I thought it would never happen."

Quietly, she shares, "I've actually wanted this for a long time now."

"You have?"

She nods. "I have."

"Well, shit, woman, if I'd known that…"

I'm bare, so I quickly get to work on the rest of her clothes—bra, panties, that damn other fuzzy pink sock.

Once I have her naked and beneath me, I peer into her eyes and stroke her hair away from her forehead. As much as it sucks, we have a quick talk about health and birth control.

But as soon as that's out of the way, I tell her, "You're so fucking beautiful, Ellie. I don't mean just here." I caress her soft cheek, her perfect full lips. But then I drop my hand to her heart and say, "I mean *in* here, as well, where it matters most."

"Nils," she chokes out, tears welling in her eyes. "I lo—"

"Shhh." I hold my index finger to her lips. "I know what you're going to say, and my heart is bursting to hear it from you. But I want to be the one to say it first."

She nods, and I move my finger from her lips so I can tell her, "I love you, Ellie Troy. You own my fucking heart and soul."

"Nils, I love you too." Tears stream down her cheeks, but I swipe them away with my thumbs.

She then murmurs more words that are a salve to my soul. "I love you, I love you, I love you."

Our hearts and souls feel joined. There's only one thing left to do to seal our love and our bond—join our bodies.

I can feel that she's ready, so with one shift of my hips and a quick adjustment of my hard cock with my hand, that's what we do.

Chapter

Nineteen

ELLIE

Nils loving me is everything I ever hoped it would be and more. He's tender at the right times and rough and wild at others.

We're insatiable too. We christen the bed, the floor, and, when I tell him about my fantasy of helping him in the shower, we end up in there, acting out everything I imagined…and more.

We spend the whole night in bed and the next morning too. We get some sleep, but not much.

That's okay.

I feel amazing.

Around ten in the morning, Nils heads down to the kitchen, insisting that I stay.

A short while later, he brings me breakfast in bed, which is so freaking sweet. Buttered toast and orange juice on a wooden tray with enough to share and a little pink rose bud in a vase.

He apologizes, "I'm sorry the flower isn't real." He lies down next to me, propping up on one elbow.

"It's perfect and beautiful," I assure him as I sit up and lean back against the pillows. "I mean, it's not like you had time to run out and buy flowers."

"True." With a mischievous smirk, he reaches under the covers, trailing his hand up my leg and curving in to my inner thigh. "You've kept me busy, babe."

I let out a little gasp, warning him, "If you keep that up, you'll be 'busy' again, and breakfast is going onto the back burner."

"Fuck eating," he growls as he lifts up and places the tray over on the nightstand. Rolling onto me, he says, "All I'm hungry for right now is more of you."

Smoothing back my hair, he flutters kisses on my forehead, my cheeks, and my chin. Then he continues down my body, kissing between my breasts, over my stomach…until he's between my legs, licking and sucking and devouring my pussy until I shudder and shake with the most mind-blowing orgasm yet.

That is until he moves up my body and gives me his cock.

Yeah, this is even better.

After this new round of loving, he props up the pillows next to me and, leaning back, tells me this time was the best for him too… so far.

"So far?" I scoff. "That was so fucking good. I really don't know how much better it can get."

"Stick with me, sweetheart," he says, chuckling. "I'm always up for a challenge."

Reaching over and placing my hand on his smooth chest, I say, "In all seriousness, I plan to stick with you through thick and thin."

He sighs. "Babe…"

We decide to finally have our toast and juice.

Hell, we need some kind of sustenance.

As we're laughing and enjoying our light breakfast, our phones ding in unison.

Holding the last bite of toast halfway to my mouth, I remark, "Huh. That's weird."

"Maybe it's some kind of an emergency alert," Nils throws out, shrugging.

"I don't know about that." I pop the last of the toast into my mouth and lean over to the nightstand on my side to retrieve my phone.

Nils does the same, reaching for his cell on the stand on his side.

We pick up our phones and peer down at them at the same time.

Almost instantly, I shriek, "Shit, it's Arden."

We look up, our eyes meeting in horror. "And he's on his way over," Nils says.

"Fuck." I jump up. "We have to get dressed—and fast. He says he's in the neighborhood. It won't take him long to get here."

It's amazing how quickly two people can throw on clothes when the threat of being found out is hanging over their heads.

I've never tugged on undergarments, jeans, a sweater, and even my fuzzy pink socks so quickly.

Once I'm fully clothed, I look over at Nils. He's back in his jeans and has his flannel buttoned up over his tee.

Blowing out a breath, he says, "I think we look okay. Wait…" He reaches over and combs his fingers through my hair. "There, that's better. You were looking a little wild there."

"Oh, great." I reach up and comb my fingers through my hair, trying to make myself even more presentable. But I feel like it's a lost cause. "We are so fucked," I mutter.

"No, we're not." Nils nods once decisively. "We've got this, Ellie.

Just stay calm."

"But we didn't have time to shower," I lament. "What if we smell like sex? I mean, we've been having a lot of it."

"True." Nils glances around the bedroom, then he suddenly says, "Wait, I have an idea."

Quickly, he hurries into his walk-in closet and comes back out with a blue spray bottle.

"What's that?" I ask.

"Febreze," he says as he starts spraying it all over his clothes. "What's their motto? 'Stink out, freshness in'? I think it's something like that. Anyway, we should be good if we use this."

I remind him, "But our clothes aren't the problem, Nils. *We* are."

"Nah." He hands me the bottle. "I'm telling you, this shit covers up everything. I've even sprayed my gear with it."

I raise a brow. "And it worked?"

"It did."

"Let's hope you're right," I murmur softly as I spray away.

When I feel that I sufficiently smell like fresh laundry, I nod. "Okay, let's do this. Hopefully, Arden won't suspect anything. I'm not ready for his wrath. I mean, I know he'll have to find out about us eventually, but not yet."

Nils agrees that now is not the time to hit him with the news, and then, sucking in a few final sobering breaths, we head downstairs.

Just in time, too, as the doorbell is ringing.

"Oh, geez." I cringe. "I think he's going to know."

"No," Nils insists. "We're fine."

As he walks over to open the door, I stand at the base of the stairs, trying to casually lean against the banister as I plaster on a fake smile.

Yeah, like this doesn't look suspicious.

Nils is much calmer than I am. He lets Arden in, and they do some kind of shake and bro-hug thing. They then engage in a quick discussion about Nils's ankle.

From the entry hall, Arden finally notices me standing randomly at the base of the stairs. "Hey, Ellie," he says, eyeing me up and down.

Oh God, I hope I don't look too rumpled.

"Hey." I rush over to give him a hug, mainly so he'll stop looking curiously at me.

It's more personal than the barely touching bro-hug he had with Nils, so I'm not totally surprised when, letting go and stepping back, he says, "Wow, you smell like…what's that stuff called again? Oh, I know—Febreze."

Oh, great.

Well, at least he didn't say "sex."

With a quick narrowed-eyed side glance to Nils, I try to sound casual as I explain to Arden, "Yeah. I wore this sweater yesterday, and it still looked clean. But when I put it on, I wasn't so sure. So I sprayed it with, you guessed it"—I point at him like he just won a prize—"Febreze!"

"Huh." He frowns a little, like he knows something is off. "Okay."

Looking at me, then at Nils, then back to me, he asks, "So, what were you two doing when I texted?"

Shit, really?

Nils stifles a cough, and I freeze.

"I was in the kitchen having some toast," Nils says at the same time I blurt out, "I was eating breakfast with him."

That would be fine and line up with his answer to Arden's question, except my stupid ass just pointed up the stairs.

Arden looks past me to where the freaking *bedrooms* are, eyebrows knitting.

Before he can question us—or, worse yet, put two and two together—I hurry up and divert the whole conversation by saying, "Hey, I haven't told you yet, but I made a decision about my future."

That gets his attention.

Phew!

He's looking at me again, not up toward the bedrooms, as he asks, "Wow, no way. What did you decide?"

Throwing my hands up in the air like I'm doing some kind of a crazy cheer, I say, "I'm staying in Atlanta!"

Arden ignores my theatrics—thank God—and just replies warmly, "That's fantastic, Ellie."

He comes in for another hug, and all I can think is I hope the Febreze is still doing its thing.

When he lets go and steps back, he smiles and says, "This is so great. I mean, really fucking wonderful. In fact, it's so good, I think we should go out to lunch to celebrate." His gaze pivots to Nils. "What do you think, man? You should come along too. We can also celebrate how well your ankle is healing. Good news all the way around."

"Sure," Nils replies. "Lunch sounds nice."

"Yeah," I chime in. "That'll be fun."

I hope.

The timing's not great, but I guess this little impromptu outing should go okay. I'd prefer to talk with Nils alone first, so we don't have any more screwups like the breakfast thing.

But it looks like that's not going to happen, seeing as Arden just turned to the door and said, "Cool. Let's go."

But then, before anyone moves, Arden's phone starts ringing.

Yes!

Saved by the bell...or ring, like literally.

He looks down at the screen and says, "Hey, guys, it's Willow. Let me take this outside. I'll be back in a minute."

Once Arden steps out, Nils and I look over at each other and, shoulders slumping, blow out simultaneous relieved breaths.

"Oh…my…God," I say. "I can't believe I almost blew it when I freaking looked up the stairs and said we were having breakfast *together*. Ugh!" I place my hand on my forehead and shake my head. "I don't know why I did that. It was some kind of a Freudian slip, for sure."

Nils says, "Ah, don't worry about it. You were just caught off guard. You recovered quickly, though, with the news that you're staying in Atlanta."

"Yeah, but now Arden wants to go out to lunch to celebrate. Are you kidding me? Nils…" I give him a stern look. "We have to be really careful."

Shrugging, he says, "Maybe we should just tell him about us at lunch."

"I don't know," I hedge. "I sort of wanted to be the one to tell him. You know, in case he's really mad. That way I can bear the brunt of his anger. Then I can explain to him that it's not just some hookup fling-type thing."

"Nah." Nils shakes his head. "We should do this together, Ellie. And you're right—it's not a hookup fling-type thing. We're a couple now."

Though we've professed our love, and I know we're "together," it's nice to hear him say the words.

"Are we a couple?" I ask, just to hear him say it again.

Laughing and shaking his head, he says, "You're funny. You know we are. I love you, and you love me. That pretty much says it all right there."

"Yeah, it does." I smile, wishing I could go over and give him a hug. But Arden will be coming back in any second now.

In fact, just as I'm about to say, "Maybe we should just get it over with and tell him at lunch, after all," my brother steps back inside the house.

He doesn't look happy, so I ask, "What's wrong?"

"Oh, it's nothing terrible." He waves his hand. "Willow was shopping up by our house, and she came out of the grocery store and noticed she has a flat tire. She called for road service, but I'm going to head up there anyway and wait with her. So..." He blows out a breath. "It looks like we'll have to postpone that lunch."

Relieved, because maybe this is the universe telling Nils and me that we definitely should wait to say anything to Arden about us, I hurry up and say, "No worries. We'll celebrate another time."

"Okay, but soon." Arden points at me, then at Nils as he adds, "I'm not waiting too long to celebrate with two of my favorite people."

Yikes, I hope he'll feel the same way once he finds out two of his favorite people are in a relationship behind his back.

Chapter

Twenty

NILS

We successfully keep what's now our secret relationship from Arden. But what I told Ellie is true—I think we should tell him together.

I mean, how mad can he be once he knows we're in love?

This isn't some random fling.

This is the real deal.

Unfortunately, though, when two people are so in love and into each other, like we are, time gets away from you.

Another week passes, and we put our plan to tell Arden about us on hold. He's busy with away games anyway, and we still have that lunch to do.

That's fine.

I'm busy falling deeper and deeper in love with Ellie. We spend so much fucking time together, laughing and loving. It keeps me occupied while my ankle heals, and the next thing I know, I'm cleared to skate.

Yes, life is almost perfect now!

In fact, it will be perfect once I can play again.

Oh, and once Arden knows about us.

After I'm cleared, I'm allowed to practice with the team, which is fantastic. I have to wear a no-contact jersey, but that's okay with me. It feels so fucking good to be back out on the ice with a stick in my hand.

After one of our practices, I'm walking out to my car with Arden, and he mentions lunch again. This time, however, he tells me he has a better idea on how to celebrate.

"Oh, yeah? What's that?" I ask as we approach my Range Rover.

His car is in a different area of the players' lot, but he stops with me by mine.

Raking his fingers through his dark hair, still damp from his after-practice shower, he says, "I was talking with Willow, and she'd like to join us. So, what about a dinner instead of lunch? We were thinking tomorrow night, if that's good with you?"

Hmmm, if Willow is there, maybe we won't tell Arden about us. I'm not sure if Ellie prefers to hit her brother with the news while he's alone or if she'll be cool with Willow finding out at the same time.

I need to ask her, but for now, Arden is waiting for me to say something.

Mustering up some excitement, I nod and say, "Yeah, dinner tomorrow sounds great. It'll be fun going out the four of us."

"Yeah, it'll almost be like a double date," Arden says, chuckling.

I look at him and swallow hard.

Could he be okay with the idea of me and his sister dating?

I'm feeling elated that he might be, until he busts out into laughter and says, "Just kidding."

Oh God, we are so fucked.

I'm dying a little inside, but I laugh along with him. "Yeah, that was a good one," I mutter.

He tells me he'll text Ellie to verify she's on board with dinner. "In fact," he says as he takes out his phone, "let me create a group chat for the four of us. This way we can decide on a restaurant and a time."

I nod. "Okay."

So now, not only are we going on what really will be a double date from Ellie's and my perspective, but we're also now all in a group chat.

One thing's for sure: dinner tomorrow should be interesting.

When I get home, I find Ellie in the living room with her e-reader.

When she looks up and sees me, she lowers the device and sets it on the coffee table.

As I walk over to the sofa, I notice her phone is next to where she put down the e-reader.

Nodding to it, I ask, "Did you get the text from Arden?"

She laughs. "You mean the one he sent in the group chat he created?"

I roll my eyes. "That would be the one."

She chuckles. "Yeah, I got it."

After giving her a kiss on the top of her head, I sit down beside her on the sofa.

"So," I begin, "are you okay with this dinner idea tomorrow night?"

She shrugs. "Sure, it sounds nice."

Meeting her eyes, I ask, "What are your thoughts on telling the two of them about us? Should we still say something with Willow there? Or should we wait until another time with Arden alone?"

She sighs as she picks off a piece of lint from her black leggings. "I don't know, Nils. I guess the best course of action at this point is to play it by ear. If the timing feels right, then let's tell them. But if not..."

"We'll wait," I finish for her.

"Yeah, then we'll wait."

Chapter

Twenty-One

ELLIE

Dinner plans are made, and our "date" night with Arden and Willow is set. But even as Nils and I are driving to the French restaurant we let them pick out, we're still not sure if we should divulge the news that we're a couple and are madly in love.

"Are we still playing it by ear?" Nils asks when we stop at a red light about five minutes from the restaurant.

Our hands are joined on the console, and I give him a light squeeze. "Ugh," I groan, "I don't know. Part of me just doesn't feel like saying anything at all. Not tonight."

Glancing over at me, he says, "I'm fine with waiting."

The light turns green, and as he hits the gas, I blow out a breath. "You know what? Let's just wait. I want to enjoy a nice dinner with my brother and his girlfriend with no added pressure."

Nils looks as relieved as I feel as he says, "Sounds good to me."

We are clearly both putting off the inevitable. I hope it doesn't bite us in the ass.

For the rest of the drive, we just chat about mundane things, laughing here and there.

And then we reach the restaurant.

We decide to valet, but there's one car in front of us. While we wait, I check out the modern, sleek glass-and-steel facade of the building and take in all the high-end cars in the parking lot.

"Wow," I say to Nils, "Arden said this place is nice, but I didn't think it was this fancy. I'm glad I wore this pretty cashmere dress and heels."

"It is upscale," he replies as he ducks down to get a better view. "Good thing I went with a suit and tie and not the dress pants and button-down I was thinking of wearing."

"Yeah, good call."

I don't tell him, but I'm actually glad he went with a suit and tie as well. He's so damn hot and sexy when he's dressed to the nines.

After the valet attendant gets to us and takes over the Range Rover, we make our way into the restaurant.

The host just inside the entranceway takes our names and, upon checking the reservation, informs us that the rest of our party is already seated.

As we follow him to a private table in the back, Nils leans in and whispers, "I thought we were on time."

"We are." I roll my eyes and chuckle. "This is just typical Arden. He loves to be early."

"Hmmm," he says with a nod. "That sounds about right. He is usually one of the first guys out on the ice at practice and warm-ups."

I laugh. "That sounds about right."

As we approach the table, I notice Arden and Willow are dressed quite nicely too. My brother has on a black suit similar to Nils, and

Willow is wearing a pencil skirt that's a shade darker than my blue cashmere dress, along with a white blouse.

Arden stands when he sees us.

He greets us warmly when we reach the table, giving me a hug and Nils a handshake.

"Ankle still feeling a little better each day?" he asks Nils.

"Yeah," Nils replies, nodding. "I think I'm going to be cleared to play soon."

Smiling, Arden tells him, "That's fantastic."

"That is great," Willow says, jumping in.

She stands and comes over to hug Nils, then me.

Stepping back, her hands still on my elbows, she says, "And you, I heard the great news that you're staying here in Atlanta. I'm happy you're not leaving town, Ellie."

"I am too," I reply honestly. "It just feels right to stay."

"No second thoughts, then?" she asks.

I shake my head. "Not a single one."

She glances over at Nils, almost kind of knowingly, as she says to me, "Almost like it's meant to be, huh?"

Nils and Arden are busy talking as they take their seats, so I catch her gaze and say softly, "I think it is."

"Hmmm," she hums noncommittally.

I sense she's onto us.

You know, women's intuition and all that.

Willow and I take our seats, and, after we're settled, we all begin perusing our menus.

When the waiter comes over to take our orders, we're ready.

We each order the salade Niçoise and a large coquille appetizer to share. For our entrées, I choose chicken cordon bleu, Nils orders beef bourguignon, which is a kind of French beef stew, and my brother and Willow both go with poached salmon with Hollandaise sauce.

With our orders in, the conversation flows freely. We all laugh and have a good time.

The courses arrive one by one, and we end up sharing bites of our entrées with one another.

"This salmon is amazing," I remark.

"It is good," Willow says. "And I'm in love with your cordon bleu."

The guys jump in with their own commentary, and the consensus is that everything is beyond delicious.

After we're done with our meals, we decide we're too full for dessert, but we do opt for coffee.

There are more comments about how wonderful dinner was and how we'll have to do this again, but I can't help but notice that Arden and Willow keep smiling at each other like they have something to share.

Finally, Arden clears his throat, then, with a big smile, announces, "Hey, we have something we want to tell you guys. We discussed it on the way over and feel like tonight is a good time to share our news."

From Arden's big smile and the way Willow is blushing ever so slightly, I have a feeling she's either pregnant or they're getting engaged.

I'm humming with excitement at the prospect of either—or both!—when I say, "Well tell us!"

Laughing, Arden says, "It's not official-official—'cause we're having the engagement ring designed and it's not ready yet—but I asked Willow to marry me."

"And I said yes," Willow blurts out excitedly.

"Oh my God!" I'm practically bouncing in my seat. "I am so freaking happy for you two. This is fantastic news!"

I truly am beyond ecstatic for my brother and Willow.

Nils reaches over and shakes Arden's hand. "Congratulations, man."

"Thanks."

Nils raises his coffee cup and says, "We don't have champagne, but let's toast the good news."

"Hear, hear," my brother says as we all clink our cups.

What a perfect, perfect night.

Chapter

Twenty-Two

NILS

On the way home from the restaurant, Ellie is humming with excitement for her brother and Willow. Her enthusiasm is contagious. I keep smiling and agreeing with her that their news is "awesome."

I'm happy for them too. It's good to see my friend has finally found his life-mate.

I don't say anything, but I have a feeling that I've met mine too.

No, I know I have.

Too bad it's still a secret, though.

But we made the right decision not to say anything about our relationship status tonight.

Ellie must be thinking along the same lines, as she says, "Good thing we decided to wait to tell them about us."

"I was just thinking that," I share as I slow to a stop at a red light.

"Yeah." She nods contemplatively. "They deserved to have their moment. If we had said something first without knowing any better, they probably wouldn't have even told us about their engagement."

"Maybe not," I agree.

The light turns green, and I accelerate. Ellie looks like she's mulling something over, so I ask, "What's on your mind?"

Letting out a sigh, she says, "I was just thinking that we should probably wait a little longer before we say anything about us. I don't want to piggyback on their news, like we're trying to steal their thunder or something."

Since it's her brother, not mine, it's her call.

I tell her as much, then add, "I don't think Arden or Willow would think that, though."

She sighs. "No, you're probably right. But I want to be considerate and still wait."

"Then we'll wait, sweetheart," I say as I reach over, take her hand in mine, and raise it to my lips to deposit a light kiss.

As I lower our joined hands to the console, we reach our house. I pull into the garage and realize it's become exactly that—*our* house.

And that reminds me that there's one thing we've not addressed— where does Ellie plan to live now that she's staying in Atlanta?

I want her to live with me, but if she's set on getting her own place, that's her prerogative.

I'll have to respect that.

A wave of sadness comes over me thinking she might leave our house, and I let out a long, resigned sigh.

Looking over with concern, Ellie touches my arm. "What's wrong, Nils?"

I love how we can so easily read each other's emotions. And we're always honest with each other, so, cutting the engine and lowering the garage door behind us, I push my seat all the way back, because here is as good a place to talk as any.

I pause for a beat, listening to the sounds of the engine cooling down.

And then, tapping my hands once on the steering wheel, I guess to steel myself for if she wants to live on her own, I say, "There's something I'd like to discuss."

The timed light that came on when we entered the garage flicks off, and we're left in the shadows.

"What's that?" Ellie asks quietly, as if the darkened garage requires soft voices.

With my eyes adjusting to the near-darkness, I look over at her and say, "We haven't talked about where you plan to live now that you're staying in Atlanta."

Biting her lip, she says, "That's because I haven't really worked out that part."

It's silly that I feel nervous. I mean, fuck it, we're in love.

But I still need to draw in a deep breath and release it before I ask, "Would you want to stay here and live with me?"

My eyes flick to hers, then away.

Fuck, what if she says no?

But she doesn't.

Instead, she lets out a little laugh and mutters, "Silly man," as she kicks off her heels and climbs over the console.

"What are you doing?" I stupidly ask as she hikes up her dress and places her knees on either side of my thighs.

Lowering onto my lap, she takes my face in her hands and says, "I'm telling you yes, I'd love to stay here and live with you."

A gush of relief washes over me, and I wonder why I was ever really worried.

Living together already feels so natural.

Why would we change a thing?

Laughing, I reply, "Well, this is one hell of a way to say it. But I like it." I place my hands on her bare thighs and slide them ever so slightly under the hem of her dress. "I like it a lot."

Since I have her in this position, we may as well make the most of it.

"Mmmm, I like it too," she hums.

"I bet you do," I say with a chuckle as I move my hands another inch higher.

Sucking in a breath, she rasps, "To be honest, I've been kind of hoping you'd ask me to stay."

I stop. "You have?"

"Uh-huh," she replies, sounding distracted now as she tries to push in even closer so my hands will go higher.

But I don't let her.

I keep my grip firmly in place.

Letting out an angry groan, she huffs and calls me out. "You're a tease, Nils."

"You've got that right, babe." I lean in and, tucking back her hair, whisper in her ear, "I'm going to make you so fucking hot you'll beg for me."

I'm playing it cool, but I'm hard as fuck right now.

Looking down, she sees my cock tenting my pants and lets out a lusty, need-filled groan.

"Do you want that?" I ask as I slide my hands under the hem of her silky panties and squeeze her bare ass cheeks.

She grinds into me as she gasps, "Fuck yes."

I'm careful not to let her get down low enough to use my dick to get off on.

No, I'm going to be the one to do that.

"Nils," she cries out, "please."

"Please, what, babe?"

"Touch me. Do something."

So I do—I rip her thin panties down the back and toss them aside.

"Yes," she hisses. "More."

I give her more—one finger, then two, while my thumb works her clit. She's so fucking wet as she rides my hand that her pussy juices drip down to my wrist.

And that's when I know I have to taste her.

With my seat back as far as it can go, there's a good deal of room. Still, it's tight as I lift her so her hot little pussy is in my face.

Gently, I lean her back against the steering wheel, and when my tongue touches her pink nub, she moans, "Nils… God, Nils."

"Not God, baby, just me," I breathe against her sex. "What is it that you want?"

"I want more."

"Beg me, Ellie."

"Pleeeeease…" She pushes into me, 'cause she's greedy for my mouth, my lips, and my tongue.

I relent, using all three as I hold her in place while I lick and lathe and taste and kiss…

But when I know she's close, I pull her back to me.

She lets out a yelp of surprise at the loss of my warm mouth.

Quickly, so fucking quickly, I unzip my pants and lower them some. Good thing I went commando tonight, because I have her down on my cock in five seconds flat.

And then I'm fucking her—hard.

When I let up, she rides me, slowly at first, then fast, faster.

Ahhhh, this is heaven.

I pull her soft sweater dress up high enough that I can unsnap her bra. I knead her luscious breasts, sucking one nipple into my mouth, then the other.

That's when she falls apart, coming so hard that her pussy strangles my cock.

And that's it for me—I let go and pour into her.

Breathing hard, she lowers her head to my neck as I wrap my arms around her, holding her so close that our hearts feel like they're beating as one.

Ellie toys with the ends of my hair while I caress her back.

No words need to be spoken.

Our slowing breaths and gentle touches say nothing and everything all at once.

This is what love feels like.

I don't think I've ever felt this content in my entire life.

The only thing that would make things better is to share with the world what Ellie and I have become to each other—everything.

But first we have to tell Arden.

Chapter

Twenty-Three

ELLIE

The next few weeks are a whirlwind. Nils is cleared to play, and life goes back to normal.

We're in love, and our relationship is growing stronger every day. The only thing still hanging over our heads is that no one knows we're a couple.

No, wait, Finn knows. We didn't say anything to him. He guessed and then flat-out asked Nils.

He couldn't lie to Finn, so that was that. To his credit, his teammate has made a solemn promise not to say a word to anyone.

And he hasn't.

There are times that I think Willow knows too. She has that intuitiveness about her. I just get the feeling that she's onto us from her knowing looks and little smiles. Still, she's respectful. She doesn't ask, nor does she say anything to Arden. I think she respects that it's our story to tell.

And tell we must.

But not tonight. I have to work at Boots, and Nils has a home game against St. Louis.

Sitting down on the edge of our bed as softly as I can, since Nils is taking his pregame nap, I pull on one high black boot, then the other.

I already have the rest of my "uniform" on—short red-and-black plaid skirt, boy shorts, and a white blouse. I don't unbutton the shirt as low as I used to. I could tell it bothered Nils.

He never said anything, but I took action on my own.

That's what you do when you respect each other.

Nils lets out a light snore, but remains asleep.

I blow out a breath.

Though it's almost time for him to get up, I've been careful to move around the bedroom quietly and not make a lot of noise as I was dressing. I didn't get to talk to him earlier, since I was out grocery shopping when he got home from their optional practice this morning.

He's stirring, though, so we'll have a chance to catch up now.

"Hey," Nils mumbles groggily as he props up the pillows behind him, leans back, and crosses his arms over his wide, bare chest.

Unfortunately for me, he has on lounge pants. Otherwise, I might ditch my own clothes and jump on him.

Catching up could always wait for later.

But no, this is my chance to talk with him.

I need to take it.

Sexy times must be put on hold.

"I didn't wake you, did I?" I ask as I zip up my boots.

"No." He runs his fingers through his messy hair, yawning. "It's time for me to get up. I have to get ready to go."

Sighing, I lament, "I wish I could come to the game tonight and watch you light it up. You've been playing so well lately."

"Aw, babe, thanks." Tossing the covers back, he gets up and struts over to a chair where he picks up the tech tee he must've thrown over the back before his nap.

Tugging it over his head, he says, "There's always Tuesday's home game."

"Don't worry," I reply. "I'm definitely coming to that one."

"Good." Frowning, he says, "Hey, there's something I need to tell you about tonight."

I cross my legs as I ask, "What's that?"

"It's nothing bad," he prefaces. "I mean, it could be." He switches out his lounge pants for his jeans, shrugging as he zips them up. "But let's just play it by ear."

"Good God, just tell me already," I say with a huff.

He blows out a breath too. "Okay, so some of the guys were talking this morning after our practice about going out tonight after the game."

"Oh, no, I think I see where this is going." I shake my head. "Let me guess. Boots is on the list."

Leveling me with a hard stare, he says, "It's not just on the list, Ellie. It's at the fucking top."

I murmur a sarcastic "Great." And then I add, "Too bad it's too late for me to call off."

He crosses his arms. "You shouldn't have to. It was only a few guys who said they'd be up for going, and Arden wasn't even at practice. If they do decide to go, I'll text you. Oh, and..." He gives me a stern look. "I'll be coming along with them."

I roll my eyes. "Nils, I'm sure I'll be fine. I'll just make sure I don't wait on their table or stay in their section. I can switch with one of the other girls if I need to, no problem."

"I know you got this," he says. "But if I'm there, I can help keep them away from you. We don't want anyone seeing you and telling Arden you're working there, right?"

He has a point, so I concede, "No, definitely not."

This day was bound to come. Boots is a popular spot. I've been lucky that none of the Thunder players have come in before. Maybe some have. If so, it was obviously on a night I wasn't working.

But I'm working tonight.

And it sounds like their minds are made up to be at the same place I'll be.

Crap.

Boots is packed and humming. It already feels like I've spent my entire shift running around nonstop.

Actually, I have.

But now I have a quick ten-minute break, thank God.

I head to the dark-paneled employee lounge in the back. It's empty at the moment, a testament to how crazy busy it is tonight.

Relieved to get off my feet for a short while, I plop down on one of two plushy red velvet chairs situated around a low table.

Blowing out a breath, I kick my feet up onto the table and take out my phone.

I had it tucked in the waistband at the back of my skirt with the sound turned off. It was quiet all night, meaning no vibrating. That was, until the past few minutes.

Just as I was wrapping up with my last table before this break, it started buzzing.

Sure enough, I see I have a few texts—all from Nils.

Nils: *Game's over, we won. I got an assist on a goal. That's the good news. The bad news is some of the guys are still set on going to Boots tonight. I tried to suggest a few other places, but it was a no-go. Looks like I'll see you soon.*

Nils: *We're all just about ready to leave. Just finalizing who all wants to go. Finn is in, so he'll have our backs too.*

Nils: *Fuck, babe. Arden wants to come along now. This is crazy. He never wants to go out with the guys. Is there any way you can end your shift early and go home?*

After I read the texts, I lower my feet from the table, lean forward, and place my head in my hands.

Fuck.

There's no point in even replying to Nils. I can't leave work. Besides, his last text was ten minutes ago. They're probably almost here.

"Shit, shit, shit," I mutter into my hands. "I am so fucked."

Suddenly, I hear Sammie ask, "What's going on, Ellie? Why are you 'so fucked'?"

I look up, and, man, am I glad she just walked in. I need a friend to confide in.

After she sits down across from me in the other red chair, I explain the situation to her.

Biting her lip, she asks, "Your brother has no idea you work here?"

I shake my head. "No, and he won't like it. He's the stereotypical overprotective older brother. But he'll really be disappointed if he finds out by catching me here." Running my hand across my forehead, I lament, "I should have just told him a long time ago."

"Well, it's too late for that now," Sammie says. "But I think I can help."

"Yeah?" I'm genuinely curious and hopeful. "What are you thinking?"

Crossing her legs, she says, "It's easy. I'll just cover your tables for you. You stay here in the break room until they all leave. While they're here, though, I can run in periodically and keep you posted."

She's being so nice, and I appreciate it so much. Her plan is ideal, but I feel bad putting so much on her, especially with how swamped we are.

I let out a sigh. "I don't know, Sammie. We're so busy tonight. I feel like this is asking a lot of you."

"Look," she begins, "I've seen it way busier than this. I can certainly handle tonight's chaos just fine. Not to mention"—she points at me—"you're not asking for anything. I'm offering. The other girls will understand, too, once I fill them in."

I'm cautiously optimistic.

It sounds like this could work, but I'm concerned that our boss won't approve, so I say softly, "What about Annie? She's going to be pissed if she sees I'm just chilling back here in the break room while you guys are out there busting your asses."

Chuckling, Sammie says, "Actually, you have nothing to worry about. As luck would have it, Annie's son called and needs a ride home from some evening school function. I guess his friends ditched him or something to that effect."

Now even more excited that this may actually work, I say, "Really? So Annie's gone?"

"She is." Sammie nods. "For a little while, at least."

Relieved, I slump back in the chair and blow out a breath. "You really are a great friend," I tell her.

And she is.

"Just relax," she says, smiling as she stands up. "Hang in here. Like I said, I'll pop in and give you updates when I can. But don't worry. I've got this covered."

Damn, I think before I text Nils with an update about what's going on, *I hope she's right.*

Chapter

Twenty-Four

NILS

Right before a group of seven of my teammates and I walk into Boots, I receive a text from Ellie.

I read it surreptitiously as we're led by a hostess back to a large round table near the rear of the establishment.

Ellie informs me that though she can't cut her shift short, like I asked if she could, she's going to stay in the employee break room while Sammie covers her tables.

It's not ideal, as I'd rather she head out of here and make her way home, but this is better than having her out in the actual dining area, waiting on tables.

As I take a seat between Arden and Finn, I text back, *Okay, sounds good. I'll keep things under control out here.*

Since I have a view of where the employee lounge is located, and I'm next to Arden, keeping things "under control" should be easy.

I also have Finn to help out. He knows the general situation, and

I'll clue him in when I can on this new update, so he can make sure Arden doesn't go wandering around and happen upon his sister.

Not that he would, but we have to be ready for anything at this point.

As it turns out, Sammie is our server, which means Ellie would have been had her friend not covered for her.

I blow out a relieved breath.

Already, we've avoided a disaster.

Sammie takes our orders quickly and efficiently, giving me a sly wink before she walks away, like she and I are in on something.

Fuck, we are. Our combined mission is to keep Arden and Ellie apart.

I'm antsy and on edge initially, but as time wears on and our drinks and dinners arrive, I'm put at ease.

My teammates and I are having a fun time. Everyone is laughing and enjoying good food and great company.

One thing about Boots—their dinners are top-notch. Most of us ordered the surf and turf—filet mignon and lobster tail. A couple of the guys, however, opted for grilled chicken instead.

In any case, we all agree that the food is fantastic.

Since usually one of us picks up the tab for everyone, and I haven't done so in a long while, I inform my teammates that tonight's on me.

Among a chorus of "Thank you, man," I raise my hand and get Sammie's attention.

When she comes over to our table, I let her know to put everything on one check and give it to me.

"Okay." She nods. "I can do that."

She stops by another table before I see her slipping into the employee lounge. She's only back there a minute or so, and then she's heading into the kitchen to pick up food for other tables.

Damn, just knowing Ellie is in that lounge—so close, and yet so far away—makes me want to jump up and fucking run to her.

Of course, I don't. I just sit and make small talk with my teammates, counting down the minutes until we can all just leave.

But then some of the guys want to order dessert, including Arden.

Great, we're stuck here a while longer.

Sammie finishes taking the dessert orders. But, before she walks off, she looks around to make sure no one is paying attention.

Since the guys are engaged in a lively conversation, she leans down and asks me, "Can I speak with you alone for a second? I have a question about the check."

I'm kind of surprised, as I have no idea what the issue could be, but I nod and, as I stand up, say, "Sure."

I follow her over to one of the computers where the servers key in their orders. Once we're stopped, she prints out something.

"What's up?" I ask.

She shows me the printout and taps on it, but I quickly realize this is just a cover. The check isn't even ours. It's like some mock-tab, probably for training purposes.

Pretending to show me something on the faux tab, she says, "Hey, Ellie wanted me to ask you if you're, as she put it, feeling adventurous?"

Chuckling, but studying the printout in case any of the guys are watching, I ask, "And just what does that mean?"

Softly, she says, "Ellie said to tell you that she thinks you should sneak back and say 'hi' to her before you leave. I think she mentioned something about a kiss too."

Damn, this is just too tempting.

So I say to Sammie, "Tell her I'll find a way to sneak back while the guys are eating their desserts."

Crumpling the phony check, she tosses it into a wastebasket next to the station.

"Great," she says loudly. "I'm glad we got that all straightened out, Mr. Sten. I'll re-key in your entrees."

Playing along as I prepare to walk away, I say, "Yeah, me too. Thanks for pointing out that error and fixing it."

On my way back to the table, it's all I can do not to break into a huge grin.

Sneaky little Ellie. She's so bad, tempting fate this way.

But that's one reason why I love her.

I'm right there with her.

I wish I could tell Finn what's going on, so he'd know that when I announce that I have to hit the men's room, which is going to be my cover to go see Ellie, he needs to keep Arden occupied.

Hopefully, though, the dessert will do the trick.

When I sit back down at the table, the sweet confections are starting to arrive.

Good.

When Arden's cheesecake is placed in front of him, I push out my chair and say, "Hey, I'll be back. I'm going to hit the men's room."

No one pays me much heed, which is what I expected. I only made the announcement for Arden's sake, so he's not wondering where I went.

I try to get Finn's attention so I can shoot him a meaningful glance or some shit, but he's busy talking to Hayden.

Oh well, I'll only be a minute or so.

Then we'll all be out of here and on our way to our homes, no harm, no foul.

One little pit stop to give my girl a kiss?

Hell, it's worth taking a chance.

Besides, I'm sure everything will be fine.

Chapter

Twenty-Five

ELLIE

It's boring hanging out alone in the break room. A couple of the other girls stopped in earlier, but for the past twenty minutes or so, it's been just me.

I guess it's too busy out there for anyone to pop in. It's even been a while since Sammie was here.

Letting out a low grumble and jumping up from my seated position, for about the tenth time so far, I start pacing back and forth.

That's when I get the brainstorm to have Sammie send Nils back.

Yes!

I mean, he can't leave without me seeing him, right?

The guys have to be done with dinner and close to taking off. I bet his teammates are all talking among themselves. Surely they wouldn't notice if Nils leaves the table for a couple of minutes. He can pretend like he's going to the men's room.

Yeah, I bet that would work.

It's risky, I know, but I already feel an adrenaline rush.

I think it's meant to be, too, seeing as Sammie just walked in.

"Hey, sorry it's been a minute. How are you holding up?" she asks.

Putting an end to my pacing, I cross my arms, face her, and reply, "Not good. It's boring as hell back here. And I feel bad everyone is working but me."

"Don't worry," she says. "You'll be back out there soon. The guys are done with dinner. I just need to check to see if anyone wants dessert. In fact, I'm about to do that right now."

Sammie starts to leave, but she turns back when I say, "Wait. I have something I need to ask you to do for me. After you're done taking the guys' dessert orders, do you think maybe you could get Nils alone for a minute?"

"Uh-oh." Sammie looks worried. "And just why would I want to do that?"

I fill her in on how I want Nils to sneak back and say hi. "And maybe give me a kiss too," I add with a mischievous grin.

"Oh, girl." Sammie shakes her head. "You are just asking for trouble."

"I know," I concede. "There's a chance we could get caught. But I don't think so. We'll keep it quick."

"You better," she warns.

"So you'll do it?" I ask. "You'll send Nils back?"

Turning to leave once more, she says over her shoulder, "I'm on it now, lady."

Damn, this girl is the best.

I'm too antsy to sit, so I resume pacing.

My heart is beating like there's a caged bird in my chest. Nonetheless, the excitement of Nils sneaking back here while his teammates are out in the restaurant, including Arden, all blissfully clueless about us, feels just too good to back out.

Besides, it's too late. I'm sure Sammie is talking with Nils now.

It feels like the time is dragging, but it's really not.

In the midst of another round of pacing, Nils walks in.

"Babe!" I'm on him in an instant, jumping into his arms and wrapping my legs around his body.

He feels so good and warm.

Laughing, he spins me around. "Wow, someone is excited to see me."

"I am," I confirm. "This is my way of letting you know."

"Mmmm, I love it. Stay like you are."

"No problem."

I tighten my legs around him, as he trails his lips along the side of my neck, making me gasp.

Pulling back, he says, "I should have come back here sooner."

"You should have," I reply. "But all that matters is that you're here now."

Brow creasing, he says quietly, "We don't have long, though."

"I know. What'd you tell the guys?"

"I said I was heading to the men's room. Arden was starting on his dessert, but I made sure he heard me."

"Good." I blow out a breath. "Then he won't be wandering around."

"No, I don't think so." Leaning in, his lips brushing over mine, he murmurs, "So, how about that kiss?"

I rasp, "Yeah, how about it?"

There's no more waiting. Nils's lips crash down onto mine. We're both so hungry for each other in this stolen moment that our kiss is wet, even a little sloppy, but fucking hot as hell.

His hands slide down to clutch my ass, as I wind my hands into his hair.

In this moment, it's just the two of us and no one else exists in the world.

Until, from behind me, a man who sounds exactly like my brother grinds out, "What the fuck is going on?"

Uh-oh.

Chapter

Twenty-Six

NILS

Shock, betrayal, hurt, anger—these are just some of the emotions I see crossing Arden's face as I peer past Ellie, her legs still wrapped around me, while I hold her up by her ass.

Arden's eyes snap down to my hands.

He swallows hard.

This can't be good.

I instantly move my hands away from Ellie's ass and up to her waist.

That's better, but still not great.

It doesn't matter. It's too late. Arden's already seen and heard it all—me kissing his sister, my hands on her ass, her fingers in my hair, and our hot-and-heavy breathing and sexy groans.

He knows what's up.

And, man, do I ever feel like the biggest, most betraying dick on earth.

Ellie slides down my body, and, standing up straight, she adjusts her short skirt.

Turning to her brother, she says casually, like we were just in here doing nothing, "Oh, hey, Arden."

He's not playing around, though.

His eyes trail down her body, assessing her outfit in a very clinical sort of way. "Do you work here?" he asks.

"Yes." She sighs. "I do."

There he goes, swallowing hard again, before he asks, "I thought you worked at Applebee's?"

Ellie nods once. "I work there too."

His tone dripping with sarcasm, Arden says, "My, haven't you been the busy girl." His eyes snap briefly to me, and I see a grimace of disgust, but then he's back focusing on his sister. "Why didn't you tell me about *this* job?" he asks.

Ellie makes a face. "Um, probably because of the reaction you're having right now."

Whoa.

One thing about this woman, she certainly stands her ground.

And it works. Arden's expression softens ever so slightly.

Blowing out a breath, he says, "Okay, fair enough."

I'm relieved that he's addressing her lack of telling him about working at Boots as opposed to the compromising position he just found us in.

Unfortunately, I have a feeling that's about to come up real soon. He's probably just covering the least important omission of the truth first.

Sure enough, his eyes slide back to me as he says, "Clearly, *you* knew all along that she works here. Yet you never thought to mention it to me."

I hold up my hand. "Hey, it wasn't my place to say anything. And Ellie asked me to keep it a secret. I knew she'd tell you in her own time."

Scoffing, he says, "Seems you two have quite a few little secrets you're keeping."

Here we go.

"Arden…," Ellie begins, her tone even as she takes a step toward him.

He holds up his hand and shakes his head, like he doesn't want her coming to him.

She stops, and he asks her, "How long has this been going on? I mean with you two, not this job."

"A while," she replies. "We were friends first, though, if that makes any difference." Arden scoffs, but she goes on. "Look, we really, really tried to keep it just friendship. But things just…happened."

"Obviously," he says disgustedly. He looks over at me, and fuck, the betrayal in his gaze. I feel like two inches tall.

Make that one inch when he shakes his head and says, "I trusted you, man."

Mustering all the sincerity I feel right now, because the truth finally needs to be told, I tell him, "Hey, I fell in love with her, Arden. I didn't plan to, and believe me, I fought it every step of the way. But sometimes fate or whatever the fuck you want to call it has other plans."

Leaning his head back and looking up at the ceiling, Arden mutters, "Fuck."

"Hey," Ellie says, jumping in. "This isn't some meaningless fling. What Nils just told you is true—we're in love. And, Arden, you have no room to judge. You fell in love with Hayden's sister, Willow. He's a teammate, just like you and Nils are. Sometimes life just throws curveballs, you know?"

She has him there, on all counts.

Arden lowers his head, and then his eyes meet hers…then mine.

I can see he's capitulating and maybe slowly accepting we're a couple.

Still, there's hurt in his tone when he asks, "Why didn't one, or both of you, just fucking tell me? It'd have been better than me walking in on you dry-humping each other."

"Okay," Ellie interjects, "first of all, it wasn't that bad." When Arden gives her an "are you serious?" look, she amends, "It wasn't great either."

Now he's just talking to her when he asks quietly, "Why didn't you tell me, El?"

"We were going to," she replies exasperatedly.

"When?" he snaps.

She lets out a long sigh, and then she says, "At dinner that night with you and Willow, we thought about telling you. We went back and forth on the way there and were going to hold off, but at one point, I almost just freaking laid it on the line. But then you guys told us you were getting engaged, and I sure as hell wasn't going to take away from your moment."

"But that was weeks ago, Ellie," Arden protests.

"I know, I know." She runs her hands down her face. "We were still just waiting for the right time. Or, really, I was. I can't put this on Nils. He was only respecting that I told him I wanted to wait. But now I realize I should have just told you everything sooner." She swishes her hand around. "I should have told you about working here at Boots, *and* about me and Nils. I was just procrastinating, and it bit me in the ass."

Arden blows out a breath, and then, brow creasing, he asks, "Are there any other secrets I need to know about?"

"No." Ellie shakes her head adamantly. "I promise you there's nothing else."

"Thank fuck for that!" he exclaims. Sighing, he goes on. "For the record, I'm not mad about you working here at Boots. That's your decision, Ellie."

Hands on her hips, she asks, "What about me and Nils?"

He doesn't outright answer, he just asks, "Does anyone know about you two?"

Now it's my turn to jump in. "Finn does," I say. "But only because he guessed and was obviously right."

Arden nods knowingly. "Ahh, so that was why he was trying to keep me talking when you left the table."

"Yeah," I say, "what happened with that, anyway? How did you end up back here in the break room?"

"Finn got a phone call and had to go out to the lobby so he could hear. I figured I'd hit the men's room before we all left the restaurant. That's how I ended up coming through *this* door."

He gestures behind him, and it all makes sense now.

"You saw me come in here?" I ask.

"Yeah." He nods. "I thought the restrooms were somewhere back here."

Things are loosening up. I can feel it. I think Arden accepts that we're a couple.

Ellie must feel this, too, since she snarks, "Wow, I bet you were surprised when you stepped through the door and saw us."

Arden snorts. "That's putting it mildly."

Softly and much more seriously, she asks, "Do you forgive me for keeping not one but two secrets? And can you please forgive Nils too? We can't help it that we fell in love."

"Ahh, man, Ellie." Arden rakes his fingers through his raven-black hair. "I just wish you both would have come to me right away. I would have understood."

She laughs. "Would you have, though?"

He thinks it over, then shrugs. "I don't know. Maybe not. You may have been right that I would have been pissed." He sighs. "But it's only because I love you so much, El. You're my baby sister, and even when we're in our eighties, I'll always feel like I need to protect you."

"I understand that," she says. "But I have to live my life."

Jerking his chin to me, but with a smartass smirk tugging at his lips, he says, "And you want to do that with this fucker, eh?"

"Heyyy," I say, pretending to be offended.

I'm not. I'm happy that he's joking around about us. I'll gladly bear the brunt of his sarcastic humor if it means we can all get past this and he accepts that his sister and I are in love.

Stepping back to stand united with me, Ellie takes my hand and says proudly, "As a matter of fact, I do want him in my life."

Arden shakes his head, but he's chuckling, so that's good. "Man, you two. Just next time you're keeping a secret, share it with me right away, okay?"

"You'll be the first to know," I say.

Ellie nods. "Yes. In fact, I'm going to start sharing *everything* with you, big brother. Like, how 'bout this one… My damn period started earlier, and I didn't have a tampon in my bag. Thank God for Sammie. She's a lifesaver, because she had lots of extras." She shrugs. "Turns out, it's her time of the month too. Anyway, that's when we realized we're synchronized! It's so cool when that hap—"

I'm laughing my ass off, but Arden is wincing.

Holding up his hand, he cuts her off. "Okay, okay, okay. You made your point. That's not the kind of stuff I need to know. Feel free to keep those details to yourself."

I'm still chuckling, filled with relief. I'm beyond thrilled that Arden and Ellie are back to getting along and bantering.

There are no more secrets, and Arden isn't going to murder me after all.

Yeah, you could say things are looking up.

Chapter

Twenty-Seven

ELLIE

After Arden walked in on me and Nils making out at Boots, we're finally able to relax and enjoy our relationship. There are no more secrets, no more sneaking around, no more going back and forth trying to decide when to tell Arden.

Yeah, you could say it's a huge relief that my brother knows.

Better yet, he fully accepts us as a couple.

Willow does too.

She called me the very next day, and we FaceTimed.

The first thing she said was "I'm so happy for you, Ellie. But I have to tell you that I knew all along you two would end up together. I felt the energy between you. You're like two halves of a whole."

She really is that tuned in. Nils and I are exactly that. It sounds corny, but we truly complete each other.

And Willow knew it all along.

Since she was so sure we were meant to be, I had to ask, "Did you suspect at any point in time that we'd fallen for each other?"

"I did," she confirmed. "I could see a change in you both, one for the better. You and Nils just seemed more content."

"I knew it!" I exclaimed. And then I had to ask, "Why didn't you tell Arden?"

She blew out a breath. "I have to be honest. I thought about it. But I wasn't completely sure. And more importantly, it's always been your story to tell. Well, yours and Nils's."

"Thank you," I replied.

The conversation changed, and she asked if I wanted to go with her to a game this week.

"It was actually Arden's idea originally," she shared. "He got us tickets in the players' girlfriends and wives section."

Ahh, now I knew he really had accepted my relationship with Nils.

Amazed, I murmured, "I've never sat in that section."

It's true. I've avoided those seats like the plague for fear that someone would realize Nils and I were more than just friends.

But now we can shout it out to the world.

We're in love!

Everyone knows now, anyway, including all the Thunder players.

So I told Willow, "Yes, I'd love to go."

We're here now, walking into the arena to watch our guys. Willow is wearing jeans, ankle boots, and a black-and-silver Thunder jersey with Arden's number on it.

I'm proudly—and finally!—wearing a jersey with Nils's number, which I also paired with jeans but, unlike Willow's, my boots go to my knees and fold over.

We find our seats and say hello to the other significant others in the section. Everyone is so friendly and nice. Some of the girls I've met before, and they congratulate me on having announced publicly that Nils and I are a couple.

I feel good, like I fit in.

I can't believe that a few short months ago, I had no idea how the next chapter of my life would unfold. I came here to Atlanta to figure it out.

And, boy, have I ever!

I'm finally at a place where I feel at peace that I'm heading in the right direction. The best and most unexpected part is Nils. So much for a fling, huh? I knew there was potential; I felt it from the start. And now here I am—in love with the man I want to spend the rest of my life with and living with him.

I've also applied to a few law schools in the area. I have no doubt I'll get in to all of them and have my choice.

When that time comes, though, I'll make the decision with Nils. That's how we roll.

We help and support each other and celebrate our "wins" together.

That's why I just started cheering like a maniac. It's five minutes into the first period, and Nils just scored.

He took a beautiful shot from the blue line, one that was only meant to get the puck to the net so a teammate could hopefully shoot it in.

But the little bugger zoomed past everyone, including the opposing goalie.

Yay!

I high-five Willow, and Nils celebrates with his teammates.

I then see him scanning our section, looking for me.

I give him a little wave, and he smiles.

Even from a distance, I see his gaze soften.

I blow him a kiss, and he mouths, "I love you."

Time stops, and for that beat, it's just Nils and me in the whole arena, one man and one woman, so in love it's not even funny.

My heart swells with emotion, and that's when I know with every fiber of my being that we're in this for the long haul, as in forever.

I see marriage.

I see children.

I see us growing old together.

Nils is my present and my future.

He is my life.

Epilogue

NILS

Six months later...

The seasons pass, and I fall more in love with Ellie Troy every fucking day. It's funny, as there was a time when I thought being in a committed relationship would affect my play in an adverse manner.

The opposite has proven true.

Shows how much I knew, huh?

That's why I don't make any big decisions without asking Ellie for her input.

Still, there's one thing I have to work out on my own—when to ask her to marry me.

I want to do it soon, as I know she's open to it. We've had the whole "we definitely want to get married" discussion.

Hell, we've even looked at rings.

That's how I was able to order one I'm sure she'll love. It's a traditional round diamond solitaire in a beautiful platinum setting.

That rock is huge, but not gaudy.

Anyway, the ring came in last week.

So, I'm set and ready to go.

I think about whether to do something big or just keep the proposal simple.

I'm not sure.

But then an idea comes to me…

Tonight, Ellie and I are returning to that same field where the holiday laser show was held last winter. This time, though, it's for fireworks on the 4th of July.

I think I'll ask her to marry me while we're there.

That place holds special meaning for us. It's where I finally surrendered, and where we first kissed.

We've been together ever since that night, so it's more than fitting.

With the decision made, I spend the rest of the day counting down the hours.

And let me tell you, tonight can't get here fast enough.

Ellie is leaning back against me, my arms are wrapped around her, and fireworks are exploding above our heads.

We're in almost the same position we were in all those many months ago, only it's not cold out, and the field is nice and grassy.

The time feels right, so just as a huge shower of red, white, and blue lights up the night sky, I slip out from behind Ellie and drop down to one knee in front of her.

"What are you doing?" she asks, looking totally confused.

Good, I want this to be a surprise.

Digging into my jeans pocket for the ring, I tell her, "Ellie, there's something I've been meaning to ask you." Before she can put it together, I pull out the ring and say, "Will you make me the happiest man on the planet and marry me?"

Her beautiful turquoise eyes widen, and then she's smiling and laughing and saying, "Yes, yes, I'll marry you, Nils."

I slide the ring onto her finger and stand up.

My lips are on hers then. I'm kissing the woman who's about to be my wife with all the love I feel for her.

And you know what?

In this moment, I really am the happiest man on the planet.

The End

Up next in this new *Breakaway Hockey* romance series of interconnected standalones is book #4—*Finn*—releasing October 2024!

About The Author

S.R. Grey is a USA Today Bestselling Author of the new Breakaway hockey series and the popular Boys of Winter hockey books and Men of Fall football novels. Other New Adult and Romantic Suspense works of hers include the Judge Me Not books, the Promises series, the Inevitability duology, A Harbour Falls Mystery trilogy, and the Laid Bare series of novellas.Ms. Grey resides in Pennsylvania. When not writing, she can be found reading, traveling, running, or cheering for her hometown sports teams, sometimes all at the same time.

Visit S.R. Grey's Author Website
(if for nothing else, because it's pretty!):http://srgrey.com/
S.R. Grey on Facebook is a hoot:http://www.facebook.com/
SRGreyS.R. Grey's FB Reading Group is even more fun:https://
www.facebook.com/groups/SRGreyHardAbsandHotBooks/
Sign-up to receive her exciting Author Newsletter (you know you
want to):http://mad.ly/signups/106801/join
Follow S.R. Grey on BookBub for selected Sales Updates:https://
www.bookbub.com/authors/s-r-grey
Follow S.R. Grey on Twitter for randomness:https://twitter.com/
AuthorSRGrey
Follow S.R. Grey on Instagram for the riveting pics (well, at least
she thinks so):https://www.instagram.com/authorsrgrey/
S.R. Grey Goodreads Author page:http://www.goodreads.com/
author/show/6433082.S_R_Grey

Wait!

It's not over yet.

Check out the first chapter of ***Destiny on Ice***, the beginning of my bestselling *Boys of Winter* hockey rom-com series.

ONE

GOLDEN BOY GETS A LITTLE TARNISHED

BRENT

My father was a great hockey player. Back in the day, in the era of eighties' big hair and synthesized music, Billy Oliver won not just one, but two Stanley Cups. He was awarded the Conn Smythe trophy both times and has received an assortment of other hardware throughout the years.

He's retired now, but my dad was once a star.

To me, though, he's always just been Dad.

But as his only child, I have a legacy to live up to. I pray I don't disappoint him. I pray someday I'll be as good as he once was. And damn it, I better win a freaking Stanley Cup like he did.

I have no choice, not really. Since the moment my father first laced up hockey skates on my three-year-old little feet, the look of pride on his face told me even then all I needed to know—anything short of being the best will never do.

And guess what?

In many ways, I've become the best at what I do, which is, like my dad, play professional hockey.

I've been good since the start, a natural some say. I don't know about that, but I do know that even before I was drafted—in the first round by the Las Vegas Wolves, an expansion team at the time—I was being called "The Golden Boy" and "The Next One."

These days, three years later, I'm pretty much the poster boy for the NHL. And I have a slew of endorsement deals to prove it.

Lately, though, I've been falling short.

And I really don't know why.

Something is missing for me in the game. Or is it something that's missing in *me*?

I blow out a breath and shake my head.

Things started out so great. Where'd it all go wrong?

I made a name for myself early on. Expansion teams usually struggle for years before posting a winning record. Not so for the Wolves. With me centering what was then a subpar line, I was still able to make us shine. We came out swinging that first season in the league.

BRENT OLIVER SCORES THE GAME-WINNING GOAL IN HIS AND THE WOLVES' FIRST NHL GAME, SETS UP TEAMMATES FOR TWO MORE

One month later, there was this:

THE WOLVES OFF TO A COMPLETELY UNEXPECTED STELLAR START

Then things started to slide.

Those subpar players on my line weren't enough to keep afloat a pretty much overall crappy team, even with me centering. The Wolves' owners and management made the necessary moves—they don't mess around when shit needs to get done.

We picked up a phenomenal winger, Nolan Solvenson. He started to play and things turned around.

ADDING SKILLED RIGHT-WINGER NOLAN SOLVENSON TO ROOKIE BRENT OLIVER'S FIRST LINE PROVING TO BE A MASTERFUL MOVE ON A MID-SEASON WINNING STREAK, THAT SOLVENSON TRADE IS PAYING OFF FOR THE WOLVES!

Another trade made at the deadline gave us Benjamin Perry. A big, strong left-handed winger, he was the final piece to the puzzle. Even with far-from-elite second, third, and fourth lines, it didn't matter. Not with me, Benjamin, and Nolan on the first line. We could *not* be stopped.

Benjamin—or Benny, as he's known to the team—is adept at using his size and muscle to check the hell out of any sorry soul who happens to be matched up against him. He simply wears other players down…and then it's a fucking scorefest. Thanks, in part, to his killer slapshot.

Together with Nolan, a sniper in his own right, we were—and in many ways still are—quite a force to be reckoned with. We destroy teams, though not as much lately. But back then, man, we were racking up so many points that the press branded us the OPS line, as in Special Forces.

THE OPS LINE'S SNIPERS OF OLIVER, PERRY, AND SOLVENSON ELIMINATE THE COMPETITION WITH EASE THERE'S NOTHING COVERT ABOUT THIS LINE'S SCORING PROWESS

We worked our reputation to our advantage. Trash-talking on the ice and taunting players became our pastimes. We also happened to get a lot of pucks in the net.

Ah, the good old days.

We still trash-talk and taunt, but we aren't as lethal as we once were.

"We just need to get back on track," I murmur to myself. "The season doesn't start for a few more weeks. I'll have my shit together by then."

I better, since I'm the captain of the team. If I go down, we all sink. And that's not fair to anyone, especially not to my linemates, Nolan and Benny. Over the past couple of years they've become my best friends, which is a blessing and a curse. It's a blessing that we play so well together, but it's a curse that we also have a tendency to fuel each other's vices.

God knows this off-season we've become far too focused on partying and women. Like me, my linemates are extremely popular. Hell, let's not mince words—we're gods. In the hockey world, it's good to be a god. Guys want to *be* you and girls want to *do* you. Multiply that all by a hundred if you're not an ogre in the looks department.

And none of us are.

Not to brag—though, I guess I kind of am—but I have the most women falling at my feet. Hell, I've had women who've wanted to *lick* my feet.

Like, literally.

There was this crazy bitch this one time…

Wait, I digress. Back to where our team is today—floundering in a sea of mediocrity.

After that first good regular season, we fell apart during the playoffs. A dirty hit that sent me flying into the boards also sidelined me with a concussion. It didn't end there. More bad luck plagued our team. Nolan went into a scoring slump, and Benny took a punishing check against the boards that broke his foot. We were knocked out of the playoffs in the first round.

I went to Minneapolis, my hometown, to sulk.

"Next year will be different," my always-positive father tried to reassure me.

He was wrong.

We missed the playoffs entirely the following year, for reasons still unknown.

Then there was the season that just ended this past spring—another disappointment.

LAS VEGAS WOLVES FOLD, KNOCKED OUT ONCE AGAIN IN THE FIRST ROUND

Needing a break from all things desert-life, I said to Nolan and Benny, "Fuck this shit."

That was over three months ago. We were in the middle of cleaning out our lockers for the summer. My linemates looked at me, confused.

And then Nolan finally asked, "Fuck what shit, Oliver? What are you going on about over there?"

"Everything," I replied, gesturing around the empty locker room. "We're done, finished. Let's get the hell out of this place for a while."

I meant Las Vegas the city—and I think Nolan was catching my drift—but Benny misunderstood.

"Dude," Benny began, "we *better* get outta here soon." He checked his watch. "We have a tee time at two."

He meant the golf game we had planned, but I was having none of that.

"Fuck golfing," I snapped. "I'm talking about *really* getting out of here. I think we deserve a much-needed break from this whole damn town."

Nolan looked intrigued. "What'd you have in mind?"

I happily shared with him and Benny what I'd been thinking about for days. "Let's head up to my house in Minnesota. We can spend the summer on the lake." I grinned, bad intentions in mind. "You know I'm a fucking rock star up there. We can party every night. Hell, we can fuck and get fucked up till training camp starts up in September."

Benny was in immediately, but Nolan had to think it over in his thoughtful kind of way.

At last, he said, "Okay, let's do it."

Since that day we've been partying like rock stars. Or, more accurately, like out-of-control hockey players.

We're still on a roll, even though it's August and we have to fly back to Vegas real soon. Until then, however, I've vowed my cool contemporary house by the lake will remain *the* place to party. It's our OPS base for debauchery, after all.

In reality, though, this craziness can't go on. We all know that.

Even wild and crazy Benny had the sense to ask me just last week, "Dude, what should we do?"

"About what?"

I was in the midst of texting a local puck bunny to see if she wanted to meet me for a quickie, so I was a bit distracted.

Benny sighed. "We gotta report to camp in a less than a month. Guess it's time to start thinking about slowing down with the girls, the booze, the—"

I put down my phone and cut him off with a raucous, "Hell no, my friend. We just need to scale it back a little."

"Scale it back in what way?" Nolan, who walked in the room just at that moment, wanted to know.

I shrugged. "Maybe have smaller parties? Maybe drink a little less?"

We all agreed to those things, but we haven't followed through. In the past seven days we've abstained from partying for all of two.

This is so not going to play well with the team. My diet is crap, and I'm nowhere near peak playing shape. Sure, my body looks all lean and cut, meaning you'd never know I wasn't ready to hit the ice rearing to go, but looks can be deceiving. I went out for a run just the other day and came back fucking winded as hell.

That was a first.

Still, I'm confident I can get back into playing shape in no time. It's the inside of my head that's kind of a mess. I just don't fucking care about winning, not anymore. I mean, I do, but I don't. Does that make sense?

Nah, it doesn't to me, either. But I better figure it out, and fast.

Where's my drive to get my shit together? Where's my commitment to winning, my obligation to my players?

I ask myself these things every day now, but I guess the answers are clouded by my drinking copious amounts of alcohol and fucking way too many puck bunnies.

Dad would be so proud—not.

Well, he would be glad I diligently use protection. I haven't gone *that* far off the rails. Still, wrapping my dick up isn't enough to keep management off my ass. My agent already informed me— this morning, in fact—that the Wolves' ownership group has a pretty good idea of what I've been up to, along with my teammates, here in Minneapolis.

I listened half-heartedly when my agent woke me up to say, "Don't blow this off, Brent. Management is *not* happy with you. There's a certain image they expect you to uphold, and you're not doing that."

God forbid I'm not the team's "Golden Boy." I'm "The Next One," remember?

Bullshit, it's all crap.

Coach Townsend called me shortly after I got off the phone with my agent. He had the same warning.

"You don't want the team to take action. You're not going to like what they have in store for you, Brent, if you keep up with this bad behavior."

"Oh, come on," I replied, laughing. "The Wolves can't fire me. And what could be worse than that?"

Coach T chuckled like he knew something.

Hmm...

"I can't worry about that shit today," I said to him. "I'll start cleaning up my act tomorrow."

"Brent..." Coach T sounded doubtful.

"Really, I will," I insisted.

That was a few hours ago. And I plan to make some changes. But maybe not quite yet.

"Before tomorrow gets here," I justify to myself, "we still have the rest of today. And that means there's time for one more party."

I stride into the second-floor living room of my house, a spacious and angled space overlooking the huge lake on my property. Peering out at the crystal blue water, I announce to Benny and Nolan, "Listen up, boys. We're having one final blowout tonight, a party to end all parties."

There's a murmur from Nolan, but nothing from Benny.

"We're going to do this one right," I go on. "We party tonight. But then, when tomorrow arrives, we're done with messing around. We start training full-on."

Yeah, right, a little voice in my head coughs out.

I look around since no one besides my guilty conscience seems to be chiming in.

It's early afternoon and the sun is bathing the room—my favorite, by the way, with the way it juts out over the lake showcasing the floor-to-ceiling windows on two sides and a massive deck with a mile-long view on the other—in a warm summer glow.

Nolan, who is lounging on an easy chair with a beer in his hand, raises his bottle. "I'm in," he says.

His words aren't the least bit slurred, even though he's been drinking straight through since last night's bash.

"And then, yeah," he continues, agreeing with me, "we'll start getting ready for camp."

Despite his ability to suck down alcohol like a fish, Nolan hasn't veered too far off course. Getting back on track won't be hard for him. He's like Mr. Discipline. And he's not fooling anyone, anyway. I caught him working out in my basement gym a few days ago. With the way he was pumping iron I suspect he's been training consistently for a few weeks now.

There's still not been a response from Benny, which is unusual. Dude's always up for a party. He's probably the worst of us when it comes to out-of-control antics.

And that's saying a lot.

"Hey, where's Benny?" I ask Nolan as I scan the shadows of the room.

He nods to a sofa that's been pushed way-ass off to a far corner.

"Oh, I should've known." I chuckle as I take in an eyeful.

Benny is sprawled out on a sofa in the shadows, sleeping like a baby. His massive chest is rising and falling in perfect rhythm with the ticking clock on the stone mantel above his head. Some puck bunny he was fucking around with last night is with him, passed out on top of him.

The sheet covering their naked bodies is hiked up just enough to afford a view of the girl's creamy thigh, which is casually slung over my linemate's muscular, hairy-as-hell leg, and positioned under his semi-exposed junk.

Chuckling at Benny's total lack of modesty, I pick up a throw pillow and lob it at his head—the one that clearly controls all his thinking.

And he scores!

As the pillow makes contact—and how could it not with a pole like that marking my target?—the sheet falls off completely. I get a quick flash of perky tits and tiny ass. And then, shit—a big honking piece of man-meat assaults my eyes.

"Dude," I snort, mock-offended. "You need to cover that shit before you blind us all."

Benny stirs to life. Sitting up, he barks, "What the fuck, Oliver? I was having the best dream ever. That is till you started tossing shit at my balls. "

Nolan lets out a low chuckle. "Only you, Benny, could find a way of using 'tossing' and 'balls' in the same sentence. But really"—he tilts his bottle to Benny's dick—"you need to do what Brent said and cover that shit up."

Throughout this entire brain-draining exchange, the girl wakes up. And damn, she looks young. Letting out a little squeak, not unlike a hamster, she gathers the sheet around her naked self and scurries off to where she seems to think the bathroom is.

I only know this 'cause she's muttering something about having to pee. But the poor girl has no idea where to go. Hamster-girl flies past me, heading down the wrong hallway, the one that leads to my bedroom.

As I rush to retrieve her, I can't help but grumble, "Why in the hell do they always think the damn bathroom's down *my* hall?"

I catch up to and redirect the girl, pointing her in the correct direction. "It's that way, sweetheart," I say in my kindest tone.

No need to be an asshole; the poor thing already looks shell-shocked. Though whether that's due to waking up in a strange house or waking up next to that monstrous thing Benny calls a cock, I have no clue.

"Thanks, Mr. Oliver," she replies.

And then she runs off.

"*Mr.* Oliver?" I shake my head. "What the fuck is up with that? If she thinks I'm old and I'm only twenty-two, then…"

Whoa, wait.

Hurrying back out to the living room and pointing an accusatory finger at Benny, I say, "That chick better be over eighteen, dude. We're in enough trouble already with the team."

Benjamin Perry is twenty-eight, but he likes younger girls. Nothing illegal, so don't get your panties in a bunch. He just happens to favor babes who either look young, or are *just* old enough.

"She's twenty-three," he replies, sounding hurt by my accusation.

"What? Five years past eighteen?" Nolan peers over at me and smirks. "Hey, Oliver, you think Benny is working up to go cougar on us?"

Laughing, I reply, "Seeing as he's on his way to fucking the full spectrum of girls in their twenties, I do indeed think he's secretly working his way up to thirty."

"Small steps," Nolan says.

"Fuck you," Benny interjects. "You're both dickheads."

I put up my hands. "Hey, don't be pissed at me. Take it up with Nolan. He started with the jokes. I only brought up the chick's age for your own protection. I'm always looking out for you, buddy."

"Yeah, you usually are," he concedes. "And thanks for that." He shoots me an apologetic grin. "You really are a good kid at heart."

I shrug, feeling a little self-conscious at being called a kid. But then I see what Benny is up to, preparing to bust my balls.

Sure enough, the next words out of his mouth are "You do know I mean *kid* in a good kind of way. Like maybe"—he smirks—"a *golden boy* sort of style."

"Ha. Ha," I retort. And since he's enjoying yanking my chain far too much, I shoot him the bird. "Shut the fuck up, man."

Benny may give me a hard time, but his underlying sentiment is genuine. What he said about me being a good guy, like a decent person, is true. Despite all the craziness of late, I want nothing but the best for my friends. And just because I've been fucking up my own life lately doesn't mean Benny's and Nolan's lives have to go down the shitter too.

Really, I probably should've never invited them to Minnesota. I should have come up to the lake house by myself. That would've been the smart thing to do, especially if my intention all along has been to piss away my career.

I don't really want that, though, do I?

No.

I just need some help in getting back on track.

But where would I find something like that?

Ah, fuck it.

"So what do you say, Benny?" I ask, back to focusing on the party. "You in?"

He stretches, covering his dick with the pillow I threw at him. I make a mental note to have all my furniture *and* their decorative accents, especially the pillows, steam cleaned.

Running his hand through his shaggy, dark blond hair, he says, "Am I in for what?"

"Party tonight," Nolan interjects in his usual no-nonsense tone. "One last blowout, and then Brent here says we're stopping with the bad behavior."

I have to laugh. Nolan is only three years older than me, but it's like he's twenty-five going on forty. He's the voice of reason in our crew.

Well, most of the time.

Not today, though. No, today he agrees to go all-out.

With the party plans full steam ahead, we get on our phones, texting and calling everyone we know.

"Tonight we party hard," I declare when we reconvene in the living room.

"Yeah," Nolan says, holding up a freshly opened bottle of beer.

"You mean hell, yeah," Benny corrects, raising the full shot glass in his hand.

"Hell, yeah," I echo, a beer *and* a shot on the table in front of me. "And just so we're clear," I add. "Tomorrow we give up the booze and the women. Tomorrow we start training for real."

The boys agree, and we drink to our plan.

Yeah, tomorrow we'll do all those things…

Read the rest of *Destiny on Ice* now:
Amazon: http://amzn.to/2gL1XC9